CHRISTMAS WISHES ON SUNFLOWER STREET

A DELIGHTFULLY FESTIVE READ

SUNFLOWER STREET
BOOK 4

RACHEL GRIFFITHS

COSY COTTAGE BOOKS

For my family, with love always

XXX

CHRISTMAS WISHES ON SUNFLOWER STREET

This winter, enjoy an uplifting story about Christmas, friendship and village life from the author of *The Cosy Cottage Café series.*

Christmas has arrived on Sunflower Street bringing snow, carols and fairy lights…

Roxie and Fletcher are enjoying his early retirement, taking long walks with Glenda and snuggling up to share romantic evenings together.

Lila and Ethan are practically living together now along with her cats William Shakespaw and Cleocatra. Willy's been up to his old tricks but this time, he brings Ethan a gift that he wasn't expecting for Christmas.

Joanne and Max are taking their time getting to know each other, but Max has something he's been wanting to say.

Will Roxie, Lila and Joanne's Christmas wishes come true?

Grab a mince pie and a mulled wine or hot chocolate and snuggle up with this delightfully festive read.

1

LILA

'Naughty Willy!' Lila wagged a finger at her cat William Shakespaw. 'That bread is not for you.'

Willy jumped off the table and landed lightly on the kitchen floor, flicked his tail then sauntered out of the kitchen. Lila stifled a giggle. Her cats knew her well and Willy would know that she was faking her annoyance if he heard her laugh, and if he thought for a second that she wasn't actually annoyed with him, he'd be back on the table helping himself to the freshly baked soda bread.

Lila's other cat, Cleocatra, was currently in the lounge stretched out in front of the log burner, enjoying a cosy morning. Cleo often slept upstairs but when the weather turned cold and the log burner was lit, she liked nothing better than to lie in front of it, basking in the warm glow.

Lila listened carefully for a moment, trying to work out where Willy had gone, and when she heard a soft meow, she knew he'd gone to greet Cleo and to snuggle next to her on the hearth rug.

She picked up the cheese and seed soda bread and checked it over to ensure he hadn't managed to nibble it before she caught him, but it looked fine and completely hair free. It was her own fault, she thought, leaving it out while she popped to the bathroom, because she knew how much Willy loved cheese and the smell of it baking would have enticed him from any part of the cottage.

The root vegetable soup was bubbling on the Aga and it smelt so good that her stomach grumbled. She'd been really hungry the past few weeks, and felt it was as if when winter had settled over Wisteria Hollow, it had brought a new appetite for her. Then again, her appetite had been so much better lately anyway. Getting over Ben (or *Ben the Bastard*, as her friend Roxie called him) and being so happy with Ethan Morris had transformed many things in her life. Who'd have thought back in the spring, when she was still performing nightly karaoke shows for one, that she'd be so happy come December and actually looking forward to Christmas? Life could change in the blink of an eye and she was grabbing hold of happiness with both hands while she had the chance.

She went to the back door and opened it, shivering with delight at the icy cold air that nipped at her nose and her cheeks. Everything in the garden looked winter ready, as if it had shut down until the new year brought spring and renewal. She looked beyond the garden then, at the fields that stretched away for as far as she could see, noting how barren the landscape looked, but knowing that it was merely on pause and that with the new year would come colour and new life. She had always found comfort in the changing seasons because she knew that whatever happened to her, the world would keep on rotating and life would go on.

A tiny brown robin landed on the bird table on her patio and sat there for a moment, performing a twitchy little dance as it checked the garden, its head constantly bobbing, its tail like a tiny fan that flickered up and down. It was so small that it made Lila wonder how it even survived, especially when the temperatures had dropped so low, but its fragile appearance was clearly deceptive, and the bird was hardy and robust. She glanced behind her, checking that neither of the cats had wandered out. One of the things about having cats was that she lived in constant fear of them catching the birds that came to the garden, although so far — thankfully — this hadn't happened. Cleo tended to prefer her food on a plate and Willy had a penchant for hunting mice and other small furry creatures, so the gifts he carried through the cat flap in the back door usually had four small legs and tiny paws. In the past, he'd left his gifts under her bed and in her bed when she was sleeping in it. The thought of the times she'd discovered them made her shudder because there was nothing worse than waking to find something wet, stiff and decomposing on her pillow or under the duvet next to her toes.

She closed the door, leaving the robin in peace, and went to the Aga to stir the soup. After tasting it, she added some seasoning and gave it a good stir. It was almost ready and would be a perfect match with the cheese bread. She hoped Roxie and Joanne arrived soon because she was looking forward to eating.

*H*alf an hour later, there was a knock at the front door. Lila opened it and smiled at her friends.

'Hello, hello!' She stepped back to let them in.

'Ooh it's lovely and warm in here.' Roxie removed her coat and boots but left the red Santa hat she was wearing on.

'Nice hat, Roxie.' Lila touched the fluffy white pompom at the end.

'Thanks. I thought that seeing as how it's December, I should start getting festive.'

'Have you made Fletcher put the decorations up yet?' Lila asked.

'Of course I have, and he's currently putting the lights on the roof.'

'That poor man.' Joanne Baker rolled her light green eyes at Lila. 'I hope he's using safety gear, Roxie.'

'He is and he's got Ethan helping him with his ladders, thank goodness, because I worry every year that my husband will fall off and end up in casualty.'

Lila nodded. 'Ethan said he was popping over to yours at lunchtime because Fletcher wanted his help with something and had asked him to take his ladders, so I guessed it might be to help with the great Christmas light extravaganza.'

Every year, Roxie and Fletcher decorated their house with lights inside and out, and every year Lila wondered if the National Grid went into a state of emergency as the lights were turned on.

Roxie shook her head. 'You can mock me all you like, ladies, but we've had the best decorated house on Sunflower Street for five years running and I'm not . . . I mean, *we're* not about to fail now. We even managed to get some tiny lights for the gate posts this year and a giant Santa for the porch.'

'It's not like that cackling skeleton that you had at the Halloween party, is it?' Joanne grimaced. 'That thing was creepy.'

Roxie frowned at Joanne. 'The children loved it if I remember rightly, and no, Giant Santa has far more meat on him. In fact, his belly wobbles like a bowl full of jelly and he has a giant—'

'Roxie! Don't tell us anymore. Some of us are innocent young ladies, you know.' Joanne sniggered and Lila smiled. Typical Joanne, teasing Roxie with her wicked sense of humour.

'I was going to say giant *sack full of gifts*, Joanne. For goodness sake, what else would I be on about. No one gets a Santa for their porch with a giant—'

'Willy!' Lila gasped as the cat dashed out of the lounge and back into the kitchen.

Lila ran after him and threw herself in his path before he could jump up on the table again. He glared at her, his tail waving from side to side, then he seemed to concede defeat and headed for the cat flap in the back door. It swung as he dived through, letting a blast of cold air into the room.

'Whatever was all that about?' Roxie asked as she and Joanne entered the kitchen, their socked feet swishing on the tiles.

'I made cheese bread and Willy has been trying to eat it since it came out of the Aga. That bloody cat keeps me on my toes.'

'I did think about bringing Glenda but every time she comes here, she seems to have an encounter with Willy and it takes her weeks to recover.'

'I know, bless her.'

Roxie's little pug, Glenda, usually went everywhere with her, but a few times when she'd come to Lila's and Willy had been indoors, he'd decided to assert his authority and terrified the poor little dog. He'd done it in the garden back in the summer too when Fletcher had brought her over and he'd trapped her in the lavender bushes. Lila had adopted Willy and Cleo over three years ago and she loved them both dearly, but she did wonder at times what had happened to Willy before she adopted him to make him so mischievous and defiant. He had a mind of his own that cat, but she knew that he loved her in spite of his naughty behaviour. After all, he regularly brought her gifts, even if they weren't things she would have chosen to receive. But he meant well, and in this case, it wasn't his fault he had a thing about cheese and would do just about anything to get it.

'Lunch smells delicious,' Joanne said as she took a seat at the table. 'And this bread. Yum!'

'I guess it's worth breaking my no carbs before Christmas rule for that.' Roxie leant forwards and sniffed the bread. 'I can just feel the pounds landing on my hips and I haven't even tasted it yet. I guess that as long as I walk or run it off later, it'll be fine to indulge now.'

'Roxie you have the slimmest hips I've ever seen.' Lila shook her head as she got a bottle of non-alcoholic wine out of the fridge. 'You certainly don't need to worry about putting weight on.'

'Darling,' Roxie wiggled her eyebrows then tilted her Santa hat on her head, 'I have slim hips because I work at it. Don't forget that fact. If I'm not careful I pile on the pounds. I swear it's the menopause because my metabolism was always very efficient but since I hit my late forties, it's slowed right down. Even though I do exercise like mad, I'm nowhere near as trim as I was in my twenties.'

'It must be awful to be so gorgeous.' Joanne tutted then twisted her wavy ginger hair and pinned it up with a clip.

'You're gorgeous.' Roxie blew Joanne a kiss. 'But thank you.'

'And who is the same as their twenty-something self, Roxie?' Lila asked. 'I know I'm not and to be honest, I wouldn't want to be. I feel much wiser and stronger now than I did back then and I wouldn't want to go through everything again just so I could have the skin and figure of a twenty year old.'

'There is that.' Roxie nodded. 'Yes, I wouldn't want to go through my twenties again. Not that there weren't good times, because there most certainly were, but because I like where I am now, and in spite of my menopausal symptoms, I am more comfortable with myself and my body than I've ever been.'

Lila took the bottle to the table.

'Help yourselves.'

'I don't think I should actually.' Joanne eyed the bottle, worrying her bottom lip. 'I'll be asleep by three if I start drinking now.'

'It's alcohol free.' Lila pointed at the label.

'Oh god, no. Whatever will they think of next? Non-alcoholic gin?' Roxie shuddered dramatically.

'Actually, that's a thing now.' Lila nodded. 'I saw some at the supermarket when I was looking for the wine.'

Joanne poured wine into the glasses that Lila had set on the table then the three of them tried it.

'Not bad.' Lila licked her lips

'Not great either.' Roxie swirled the wine around in her glass. 'I just don't really see the point. I mean . . . wine should have an alcoholic percentage to it. Otherwise, just drink water or juice, right?'

'I quite like it.' Joanne had almost drained her glass. 'It's refreshing.'

'I think so too,' Lila said.

'Anyway, Lila.' Roxie sat up straight and righted her hat like a judge righting her wig in court. 'What's this news you have to share with us?'

'Oh . . .' Lila gulped. She'd been able to push it away while getting everything ready for lunch and with Willy being naughty, but now she realised that it was still there, lurking in the shadows, making her belly flip and her palms sweaty. 'Right. That. Uhhhh . . .'

She looked first at Roxie with her shiny dark hair in soft waves around her striking face, her big green eyes like emeralds surrounded by thick black lashes and framed by her perfectly shaped brows. In black skinny jeans and a slouchy grey cashmere jumper, Roxie was elegant and classy as always. Then she looked at Joanne, her hair scraped back now, her rounded cheeks rosy, her green eyes wide open with interest, the dimples in her cheeks showing as she smiled. Joanne was wearing jeans and a T-shirt with a polar bear on it, looking cute and curvy as she always did.

Lila loved her friends. They were so different in many ways, but both beautiful, inside and out, and she knew she could tell them anything.

So why did this feel so difficult?

They'd helped put her back together after Ben had gone, had mopped up her tears, cleaned and tidied her home. Roxie had even helped her take her wedding dress and accessories to the greyhound charity shop when Lila had been torn between keeping it in the attic and getting rid of it for once and for all. Roxie and Joanne had gone through their own share of troubles, ups and downs, worries and happy times, and they'd gone through it all together, as a team of three. Lila could rely on these women to get her through anything as they could with her. When one of them was low, the others buoyed her up. It was wonderful to have such close friends and Lila was grateful every day for hers.

She cleared her throat. 'OK. Right then . . . Here's the thing.' She swallowed hard.

The cat flap flew open.

There was a flash of black and white from the floor to the table.

Two women screamed.

Glasses shook, spilling wine on the tablecloth.

'Willyyyyyyyy!' Lila jumped up but she wasn't fast enough and the cat was gone, taking a chunk of cheesy soda bread with him through the cat flap, the rest of it falling to the tiles then spinning across the floor.

Roxie went to the door then picked up the bread. 'At least it was too big for him to get the whole thing through the cat flap.' She dusted the bread off then put it back on the table and shrugged. 'Looks OK.'

Lila sighed then muttered, 'Saved by the cat.'

'Oh no you don't.' Roxie slopped more wine into their glasses. 'Come on, what's up?'

'Well, you know how sometimes you have your period and then sometimes you don't.'

Joanne thumped the table. 'Only if you're—'

'Menopausal.' Roxie sniffed.

'Yes, there's that,' Lila said, 'but there's also the other thing.'

'Are you?' Joanne asked.

'Menopausal?' Roxie knitted her brows. 'You, Lila?'

'No, not that. Actually, I think it could be the other thing, but I'm not sure and that's why I need your help.'

Over soup and soda bread, she explained what had happened and why she wasn't sure, and her friends came through for her exactly as she had known they would.

2

———

ROXIE

*R*oxie pulled into a space in the supermarket car park and cut the engine. She sat still for a moment, letting everything Lila had told her and Joanne sink in. *Poor Lila.* She didn't have any family around to support her, and over the time of their friendship, Roxie had become quite protective of Lila, caring deeply about the sweet younger woman and wanting to do what she could to help. It was why she and Joanne had come to the supermarket to get what Lila needed. Roxie wasn't looking forward to buying it, but she'd do whatever she could to be there for her friends.

'Come on then, let's get this done,' she said to Joanne.

'Lila's OK, isn't she?'

'I guess so.'

'I do worry about her not having any family around.'

'I was just thinking exactly the same thing, but then I realised that she has got family. She's got us and we choose to be there for her, unlike family members who might be there because of a sense of obligation, so that's even better. Not that her parents chose to be around for her but that's their loss and it's a very big loss indeed.'

Joanne nodded then climbed out of the passenger seat. 'Such a shame but if they're that cold then Lila is better off without them.'

They crossed the carpark then strode through the automatic doors. Warm bread fragranced air washed over them from the vents above the doors. Roxie thought about an article she'd read about it being a clever ploy to get people to go to the back of the supermarket. It made shoppers want to pick up some bread, meaning that they had to pass all the other aisles with their tempting offers and therefore they were likely to spend more. She could see how that would work because even though she hadn't long eaten lunch, she now fancied freshly baked bread.

'Shall we get some mince pies?' Joanne asked as she grabbed a basket and hooked it over her arm.

'Mince pies?' Roxie frowned. 'That's not what we're here for.'

'I know but seeing as how we are here and the Christmas hits are playing and I can smell baking, I thought it might be nice.'

'OK then, let's grab some mince pies too.' Roxie smiled. 'Because now you've made me want a mince pie.'

They made their way to the medicines and healthcare aisle first and Roxie walked up and down looking for what Lila needed. She reached for a shiny white box with a blue strip on it then peered at the information but the writing was tiny.

'Joanne, I forgot my reading glasses. What does it say?'

Joanne took the box.

'It looks quite straightforward really. Pee on stick. Stick tells you yes or no.'

'How many sticks are in there?'

'One.'

'Better get two then just in case.'

'Sure.'

Joanne got another box off the shelf then dropped both boxes in the basket.

'My stomach just flipped over.' Roxie pressed a hand to her middle. 'What if she is?'

Joanne grinned. 'It'll be so exciting. A little tiny baby to cuddle and coo over and . . . it will look just like Lila and Ethan.'

'It'll be lovely for them this time next year,' Roxie said. 'The baby will be about three months old and just starting to notice things. They'll have the tree lights on and be able to buy gifts from Santa and . . . oh . . .' She hugged herself, picturing Lila and Ethan with a tiny baby, the three of them in front of a Christmas tree with the log burner glowing as snow drifted down outside.

'I want to buy gifts for the baby already,' Joanne said as they left the aisle and headed in the direction of the bread counter.

'Slow down, Joanne.' Roxie laughed. 'We'd better wait and see if she is pregnant first.'

'Shit!' Joanne froze.

'What's wrong?'

'It's my parents!'

Joanne turned to Roxie, her eyes wide, her mouth contorted in a grimace. 'What will we tell them about these?' She gestured at the pregnancy tests in the basket.

Roxie looked around, noting that they were in the fresh meat aisle. 'Just throw something else in the basket to hide the tests.' Roxie grabbed two packs of meat off the shelf and placed them on top of the white boxes.

'Hello girls.' Joanne's mum, Hilda Baker, smiled as she approached them. 'I didn't know you were coming shopping, Joanne. I thought you'd gone to Lila's for lunch today.'

'I was. I did. Roxie and I just came to get something for—'

'Dinner.' Roxie finished her sentence.

'For dinner?' Rex Baker, Joanne's dad frowned. 'What're we having?'

As he peered into the basket, Roxie watched the colour drain from Joanne's cheeks.

'Fillet steaks?' Rex looked delighted. 'You're spoiling us, Joanne.'

Hilda knitted her brows together. 'Now, now, Joanne. Fillet steaks are expensive and . . . well . . . you're meant to be saving that deposit, aren't you?'

Joanne nodded mutely.

'She can spoil us now and then, Hilda.' Rex grinned at Roxie and Joanne, making no effort to conceal his glee.

'Rex, you're just pleased to see red meat in the basket. You know, Roxie, we're trying to limit our intake of red meat and processed foods. Rex has put on a few pounds recently and the GP said he needs to lose some belly fat.'

'Hilda! That's not what she said at all.'

'Oh no?' Hilda patted her husband's stomach. 'It's like a football under your coat.'

Rex raised his eyebrows as his cheeks turned pink. 'That's a bit mean, Hilda, especially in front of the girls.'

'I'm just being honest, Rex. If you can't rely on your wife to be honest, then who can you rely on?'

'Brutally honest.' He shook his head and placed a hand over his belly.

'Mum. Dad. Please . . . it's just some steak and it won't hurt to have a treat.' Joanne shifted the basket on her arm. 'And they're not that expensive anyway. So let me do this tonight to say thank you for being so brilliant.'

Hilda's cheeks flushed now. 'OK then, Joanne. Thank you.'

'What're we having with them?' Rex asked, apparently moving past his embarrassment. 'Peppercorn sauce?'

'Remember when Joanne used to call it leprechaun sauce?' Hilda chuckled.

'Yes! That was so funny. "Can I have some leprechaun sauce with my steak, please, Daddy?" you'd say.' Rex nodded at the memory.

Joanne rolled her eyes at Roxie. 'Yes, thanks for that, Dad. It wasn't my fault I misheard it.'

'Leprechaun sauce would be an interesting addition to a good steak,' Roxie chimed in. 'Anyway, Joanne, we'd better get the rest of the shopping and return to Lila.'

'Of course. Cat food she wanted wasn't it?'

Roxie nodded. 'That's right.' *Quick thinking there, Joanne.*

'See you later then, Joanne.' Rex gave his daughter a kiss on the cheek. 'Onion rings and oven chips would be nice.'

'All right, Dad.'

'Bye Roxie. See you at home, Joanne.' Hilda gave a small wave then led her husband away.

'That was too close for comfort.' Joanne sighed.

'It was a bit. What would you have said if they'd seen the tests?'

'The truth, I guess. My parents wouldn't say anything to anyone deliberately, but I'd be worried that they might accidentally spill the beans.'

'What if they'd seen the tests and thought they were for you?'

'Now there's a thought.' Joanne grimaced. 'That would have set them off on one. I've only just sorted myself out financially and that was mainly with their help as well as yours and Lila's. I am meant to be saving so fillet steaks could seem a bit extravagant, especially the ones you picked up, but I'll get them because my mum and dad do deserve a treat. They're so kind and supportive.'

'They're lovely people.'

'They really are.'

'Right, let's go and grab some mince pies and a few other bits then get back to Lila.'

*B*ack at Lila's, Roxie knocked on the door then pushed it open.

'Lila! It's us.'

'Come on through to the kitchen.'

Roxie and Joanne kicked off their shoes then went through the hallway.

'Here you are.' Roxie handed Lila a paper shopping bag.

'Thank you so much. I know I should have gone myself but the idea of looking for these then paying for them just made me feel . . . panicky, I guess.'

'Don't mention it. That's what friends are for.' Roxie gave Lila what she hoped was a reassuring smile.

'Imagine if you'd bumped into someone you knew though.' Lila shook her head. 'What would you have said?'

'Actually. . . ' Joanne gave a tight smile. 'We did bump into my parents.'

Lila's eyes widened. 'Oh god. Did you tell them? The thing is, I haven't even told Ethan my suspicions yet and if he hears it from someone else then—'

'Lila it's OK.' Joanne was shaking her head. 'Roxie reacted quickly and threw some fillet steaks on top of them.'

'Fillet steaks, eh? Well done, Roxie.' Lila's eyes filled with admiration. 'Does that mean I owe you for the steaks?'

'We told Hilda and Rex that the steaks were for their tea.' Roxie giggled. 'Rex was over the moon.'

'He was.' Joanne nodded. 'Mum wasn't quite as happy but she soon came round to the idea, so I'm cooking steak, chips and onions rings tonight.'

'Thank you again.' Lila placed the bag on the kitchen table then got one of the boxes out. 'You saved me having to go through the ordeal of buying them. I honestly think I'd probably have gone there and chickened out then come home without them. Then I'd have felt rubbish and worried about it all day, knowing I still didn't know whether I am pre . . . or not. Look at me, I can't even say the word.'

'Don't worry now, sweetheart.' Roxie placed her hands on Lila's shoulders. 'Either way, it will be fine.'

Lila's eyes filled with tears. 'Will it?'

'Of course, it will. If it's negative, you weren't trying anyway and if it's positive, you and Ethan love each other and you'll work it out together.'

Lila sniffed then wiped her eyes with the back of her hand.

'I hope so. I mean . . . Ethan's so lovely and we get on so well but it's still early days for us and what if this scares him away. How will I cope alone with a baby and . . . and . . .'

Roxie enfolded Lila in her arms and held her, stroking her hair and waiting for her to release her emotions so she'd feel calmer. When she stopped crying, Roxie leant back and met her eyes.

'Firstly, if it is positive, Ethan's a lovely man. He's not Ben the Bastard and he certainly won't leave you in the lurch. Secondly, if he did dare to so much as think about doing that, Joanne and I would set him straight. And we will always have your back, whatever happens. Don't forget that because it's the most important thing you need to remember.'

'Thank you.'

'Now . . . you go and pee on a stick and I'll make some tea.'

Lila nodded then headed upstairs while Roxie filled the kettle. When she turned around, Joanne had opened the other test box and was reading the instructions.

'What would happen if I peed on this?'

Roxie frowned. 'Nothing as far as I know.'

'Really?'

'Unless there's a chance that you're pregnant too.'

Joanne's eyebrows hit her hairline. 'Goodness, no! That's the last thing I need right now. However, imagine if you did it and . . .'

Roxie shook her head and gave a sad smile. She'd given up on the dream of getting pregnant years ago after losing a twin pregnancy. The chance of it happening at 48 was slim to none, so she would definitely be the one out of the three friends who would not be peeing on any sticks.

'Sorry, Roxie. That was insensitive of me.'

'Don't be daft, Joanne. It's not an issue. Years ago, that might have set me off crying but not anymore. Life deals us all our cards and mine didn't feature any babies of my own.

However, I am hoping to be an honorary aunty to any babies you and Lila might have.'

'I've never really pictured myself with children of my own.' Joanne shrugged. 'But then, who knows, right?'

'Exactly.' Roxie laid a hand on Joanne's arm. 'You never know what's around the corner and now that you and Max are getting along so well, it could happen.'

Ten minutes later, Roxie had drunk one cup of tea and was about to get up and make another, when she heard footsteps in the hallway. She looked at Joanne and Joanne's eyes widened. This was it; they'd find out if Lila was actually expecting. Why it had taken ten minutes, she wasn't sure, but she'd suspected that Lila might be preparing herself before she actually peed on the stick then preparing herself before she shared the result.

Roxie felt like a meercat as Lila entered the kitchen, peering at her, craning her neck to see her better but trying not to move her body. The tension in the kitchen was palpable and she knew Joanne felt the same from the way she was gnawing on her fingernails.

Lila shuffled over to them, her fluffy slipper boots swishing on the tiles, her shoulders hunched over, her blonde hair falling forwards and hiding her face. She slumped onto a chair and set her hand on the table. Her fingers were curled around a white plastic stick like it was a baton in a relay race.

'Well?' Roxie had to ask; she couldn't wait any longer.

'I'm . . . I'm . . . *Not* pregnant.'

Lila looked up and Roxie's heart squeezed. Her poor friend's eyes were red and swollen, strands of her blonde hair clung to her wet cheeks and her bottom lip was trembling.

Roxie went to Lila then hugged her from behind, wrapping her arms around Lila's slim shoulders and pressing her cheek against Lila's. She held Lila tight, rocking her gently, knowing how this felt.

'Lila . . . I'm so sorry,' Joanne said as she reached for Lila's hand. 'I guess we know how you feel about it now.'

Lila nodded then sniffed loudly. 'It seems that I was secretly hoping it would be positive. It's silly that I'm so upset because an unplanned pregnancy would be the worst thing to happen right now.'

Roxie didn't say anything, but she held Lila tight. Unplanned pregnancies weren't ideal, but they didn't have to be the worst thing in the world. If two people loved each other and they had others around who cared, things like this could be worked out. There was always a solution.

'Here, let me take that.' Joanne took the pregnancy test from Lila, holding it gingerly between thumb and forefinger, then set it on the kitchen dresser. 'I'll make some tea.'

'And don't forget to throw that stick out.' Roxie smoothed Lila's hair back from her face. 'We don't want anyone else seeing it.'

'Can you imagine?' Joanne raised her eyebrows and Roxie knew they were both thinking about Ethan. That would not be the best way for him to find out that his girlfriend thought she might be pregnant with his child.

'Get the chocolate chip cookies out too,' Roxie said. 'Now's as good a time as any for double choc chip and large mug of tea.'

3

LILA

*L*ila walked into the kitchen in her pyjamas, fluffy white dressing gown and slippers, feeling relaxed following a soak in the bath. It was only just gone 4.30 in the afternoon, but she'd been exhausted by the day's events so had decided to have a bubble bath before making dinner.

When Roxie and Joanne left, Roxie had made Lila promise to phone her at any time should she need to talk. Roxie understood what Lila was feeling and Lila was grateful to her friend. It was a strange predicament to be in, not having planned to try to get pregnant then finding she actually wanted to be, but the test had been negative and so there was nothing Lila could do other than get on with things. After all, apart from her feelings, nothing else had changed. She hadn't even spoken to Ethan about it, had no idea what his thoughts or feelings would be, and she still had some insecurities about their relationship.

Ethan was very different to her ex Ben, and he had treated her so much better in so many ways and yet, she still had times where she felt scared. Part of her held back at times because of her fears about scaring Ethan off. Ben had left her right before their wedding, hurt and humiliated her in ways she thought she'd never recover from. Ethan would never do that, she felt sure of it, but what if the idea of having children terrified him. Yes, they'd had conversations about children and friends who'd had children, and joked about how difficult it must be to suffer sleep deprivation and to have no privacy or money. However, the longer they were together, she found herself wondering about what it would be like to have a baby with him. Would it look more like her or him? Would it be a girl or a boy? Even twins?

It didn't matter now though because she wasn't pregnant and that was that.

She put the kettle on and got the milk from the fridge then paused. There was something she needed to do before Ethan came over. He wasn't officially living with her yet, but he spent most nights at hers now that his mum was better, and they'd discussed moving in together in the new year. The thought of falling asleep in his arms every night and having him next to her every morning when she woke made her stomach flip. She had fallen hard for him and knew that she wanted to spend the rest of her life with him.

But right now, she had to do something she'd forgotten to do earlier and . . . *That was it!* She needed to get rid of the test because otherwise she'd have a whole load of explaining to do and for what? It wasn't like there was a baby to tell Ethan about.

She grabbed the test stick off the dresser where Joanne had left it then stuffed it into the small kitchen bin and followed it with the test box that she'd brought down from the bathroom. The spare test she'd hidden under her bed with other feminine products that she kept stored there because the small bathroom cabinet was only big enough to hold toothpaste and dental floss.

The swing lid of the small bin waved at her and she realised that there was still a chance that Ethan might put something in there and spot the test stick, so she peered into the fridge for anything that needed to go out that she could stuff on top of it. There was a packet of cheese slices that looked a bit hard around the edges but she realised she could use them in a toastie for supper, so she got them out and put them on a plate that she returned to the fridge. She put the packet into the bin and rammed it down on top of the test packaging. When she took the bin out, she'd put the plastic into the recycling bin, but for now it could provide a cover for the test.

She didn't feel very good about the deception but in this case she thought it might be better to run with the idea that what Ethan didn't know couldn't hurt him. Why tell him about something that had never been in the first place? He might think she really wanted a baby and that could make him panic, when in reality, it had all been a mistake.

Tea made, she sauntered through to the lounge and sat on the squishy sofa, curling her legs under her. She yawned in the grey light of the room as twilight fell outside, tiredness making her yearn for a nap. The warm glow from the log burner filled the room, making her relaxed and drowsy.

After she'd drunk her tea, she shuffled down and pulled the throw from the back of the sofa over her legs then closed her eyes. In the log burner, pinecones crackled, woodsmoke and rosemary scented the room, and the cushion under her head gave off a faint whiff of duck feathers. When Cleo jumped up and snuggled around Lila's feet, she was already drifting off to sleep.

❋

 'Hey sleepyhead.'

Lila blinked at Ethan.

'Oh . . . hey you. I didn't hear you come in.'

He leant forwards and kissed her then smoothed her hair back from her forehead.

'How long have you been asleep?'

'I don't know. What time is it?'

'Quarter to six.'

Lila frowned and sat up. 'For about an hour then.'

'You OK?'

'Yes . . . I'm fine. I had lunch with the girls then had a soak in the bath and felt really sleepy. The fire was lit, the room was almost dark and I lay down and closed my eyes and must have drifted off.'

'Cleo's cuddled up to you.'

'I know. My furry footwarmer.' Lila looked down at the cat and smiled. 'How was work?'

'Not bad. Got lots done today.'

Ethan was currently painting the interior of a cottage on Sunflower Street. He'd been busy since he set up his painting and decorating business in the spring. Word of mouth worked well in a small village and he'd had a lot of referrals from happy clients. Business had been so good that he'd taken on an apprentice recently, an eighteen-year-old woman from the village who'd decided after a few weeks that college wasn't for her and that she wanted to work instead. Ethan had told Lila that Nina Fry was keen to learn and had a natural ability to cut in because of an incredibly steady hand. It had proved to be very useful when clients wanted a white ceiling but darker walls. However, he'd also told Lila that he didn't know if Nina would be around for long because she talked a lot about going travelling and doing things like Camp America. Nina also had a penchant, as many teenagers did now, for taking a lot of selfies and posting them on various apps, but she only did that in her break, so Ethan didn't mind as long as she left him out of them. Some of the selfies were of her with her work though, and that was, as Lila had pointed out, good publicity for Ethan's business.

'That's good, Ethan. Do you want a cuppa?'

'I'll pop upstairs to shower and change first, if you don't mind. All I can smell is turps right now.'

'Of course. You do that then I'll make us some tea.'

He kissed her softly on the lips, making her heart flutter, then kissed her forehead before heading upstairs.

Lila lay back down on the sofa, listening to him moving around. It was so comforting having another person in the cottage. The time she'd lived alone had been fine, apart from the grieving for Ben, that was, but since Ethan had come into her life, everything had seemed so much brighter. The familiar sound of his movements from bedroom to bathroom were as reassuring as a warm hug, everything she wanted and needed was right here under her roof. If she never had a child, she'd be fine as long as she never lost Ethan. It wasn't that she couldn't live without him, because she knew how strong she was and she knew she'd cope alone, it was more that she wanted him around, wanted to have him in her life because she loved him so much and would miss him terribly if he left.

When she heard the shower stop and Ethan coming back down the stairs, she got up and went to the kitchen and filled the kettle. While she was waiting for it to come to the boil, the cat flap squeaked as Willy returned.

'Good evening, William Shakespaw.' She smiled at him and he blinked up at her then meowed. 'Are you asking for your dinner?'

He stalked over to her as if he was a show pony then twirled around her legs, his long tail brushing against her pyjama bottoms. Lila filled his bowl and Cleo's with cat food then set them on the floor in the corner where they ate. Cleo appeared just as Lila set the bowls down, clearly she'd been listening from the lounge to everything Lila had said and done.

'That feels better.' Ethan came up to Lila and hugged her. 'I needed to shower and put my comfy clothes on.'

In his light grey lounge bottoms and darker T-shirt with his hair damp from the shower, he looked cute but sexy. Lila hugged him back, accepting the kisses he gave her, slow and soft then firmer. He smelt of grapefruit shower gel and his sandalwood shampoo.

'I'd better stop right now, Lila Edwards, or I'll have to carry you upstairs,' he said huskily, as he leant back to look at her, his eyes dark with desire, his mouth pink and inviting.

'Aren't you hungry?' Lila asked, knowing that Ethan was always hungry when he got back from work.

'Starving to be honest.'

'Well how about I get started on some dinner then we can have an early night?' She yawned. 'I'm tired even after my nap.'

'Sounds good to me.' He kissed her again then leant against the worktop while she finished making a cup of tea. 'You want any help?'

'No, it's fine. I thought I'd just make some toasted cheese sandwiches along with salad and perhaps some potato wedges. I really fancy carbs.'

'Perfect. Let me cut the potatoes though while you make the sandwiches.'

They worked side by side, Ethan telling Lila about his day, then her doing the same — leaving out the pregnancy test bit — and when dinner was ready, they carried it through to the lounge and sat on the sofa. Lila turned the TV on and they ate while watching a wildlife documentary.

Lila was relaxed in spite of what had happened that day because being with Ethan was easy. They were so comfortable together and yet there was a deep passion between them that made her stomach flip whenever she thought about it. It was something she'd definitely not had with Ben and she wondered now if that was because Ben had loved himself too much to ever love her. Roxie had called Ben a narcissist on many occasions and Lila could see that he had been one; time and space had given her insight into the type of character he was. In fact, Lila could admit that she'd had a lucky escape and that being married to Ben would have been far more challenging than she'd ever have wanted or deserved. But when she'd fallen for him, she'd just wanted to be loved. She'd never been close to her parents, they hadn't wanted her and had made no secret of that fact. They'd been emotionally unavailable and so she'd felt lonely for much of her childhood, only realising as she reached her twenties that it was them at fault and not her. Their indifference had made her feel unlovable and so when Ben had shown her some attention, she'd grabbed hold of him with both hands and believed she had to do whatever she could to hold on to him. No relationship could be based on such an unstable foundation, especially not with someone with an ego as big as Ben's had been. Lila's clinginess had fed that ego and made him feel invincible and all powerful and therefore able to treat Lila as he'd wanted to. A lot of the time he'd behaved as if Lila had no feelings, like she was a possession he could treat as he pleased.

Thankfully, Ethan was nothing like Ben at all and the way he treated her made her feel like she mattered, that he saw her as not just his partner but as his best friend too. Her sense of self-worth had grown during their time together and she felt whole again now, that she did deserve consideration and respect and in turn, that had made her stronger.

After they'd washed up and put everything away, Ethan made them tea and they took it through to the lounge then snuggled up under the throw. Cleo jumped up next to Lila and purred as Lila stroked her head then ran her hand along her back to her tail. The room was warm and cosy, the curtains drawn against the chilly night and Lila allowed herself to let go of the day and her fears, to free her mind of its worries and concerns, because all that mattered was being right here with Ethan.

There was a noise from the kitchen and Ethan turned his head.

'Was that Willy?'

'He went out after his dinner and I did try to call him back in, but he didn't come. I guess he went walkabout or dropped by to see one of his friends.'

'The ladies he visits?' Ethan waggled his eyebrows.

'I know, he's such a charmer. I doubt any of them have any cheese left by the time he leaves them again.'

Ethan laughed. 'Good old Willy the ultimate cheese monster.'

Something in the kitchen clanged then there was a clatter and the sound of an object rolling across the kitchen tiles.

'Oh god, he's in the bin.' Lila unfolded her legs and stood up. 'Bloody cat.'

'I'll go.' Ethan stood up too, but Lila shook her head.

'You stay there and keep it warm for us.'

Just as Lila entered the kitchen, Willy shot past her, a flash of black and white. She went into the kitchen and sighed at the mess. He had indeed been in the bin and pulled out everything from that day. She quickly grabbed the test box and the cheese packet and the other things from the floor then took them outside to the recycling bins where she separated them into tins, paper, cardboard and plastic. The items not yet recycled, like clingfilm and tissues, she left in the binbag then tied it and dropped in into the black bin.

Before she went back inside, she paused. It was a beautiful winter's evening. The air had an icy edge and the clear sky was a black velvet blanket inlaid with twinkling diamond pinpricks. There was the aroma of woodsmoke and earth in the air, a rich scent that made her think of warm cosy homes and gardens glistening with frost. Winter had well and truly arrived, and it was wonderful.

In the kitchen she washed her hands then locked the door and put the bin back in its place with a new bag inside it. She made her way back to the lounge, thinking about how good it would be to cuddle back up to Ethan, but something was niggling at her. Something had been missing when she'd recycled the plastic.

There was a pattering of tiny feet and a draft as Willy bolted down the stairs then shot past her and into the lounge. What on earth was wrong with him? She followed him, curious about what game he was playing this evening, hoping that he hadn't just taken a tiny dead creature up to her bedroom.

'Hello Willy.' Ethan's voice was warm as he greeted the cat then he laughed as Willy jumped up onto the sofa. 'Oh . . . What've you got there?'

Lila groaned. 'Not another mouse or vole, please.'

'No . . . it's not alive. Never has been in fact. However,' Ethan was frowning as he stared at something Willy had dropped in his lap. Willy was staring at it too, as if waiting for praise or an explanation, and as Lila got closer, she could see why. 'Willy! Where on earth did you get this?' Ethan held it up between finger and thumb.

'What is it?' Lila asked as a cold dread filled her veins. She staggered over to the sofa and slumped down next to Ethan, knowing exactly what he was going to say. Or at least she thought she did.

'It's a pregnancy test.' He peered at it in the glow from the log burner. 'And from the looks of it, someone's expecting.'

4

JOANNE

*E*arth to Joanne!'

Roxie waved a hand in front of Joanne's face. They were standing in a queue at a pop up Christmas market in the pretty village of Chiddingfold and Joanne had drifted off for a moment.

'What were you daydreaming about?' Roxie asked, her dark eyebrows raised.

'Oh . . . you know . . . Max.'

And she had been thinking about the handsome senior librarian, about how it had felt last night when he'd held her and kissed her. With his dark brown eyes, strong square jaw and thick black hair styled in the cute quiff he always wore, he was gorgeous. But not just on the outside. Max was one of the sweetest, kindest men she'd ever met, and he treated Joanne better than any man ever had — except for her dad, of course, and that was different anyway. They hadn't been together long, but she was looking forward to spending

Christmas with him and to seeing in the new year as his girlfriend.

'Everything still going well, then?' Lila asked.

'Incredibly well.' Joanne nodded.

'That's wonderful to hear.' Roxie smiled then adjusted her faux fur hat, tucking a strand of her black hair back underneath it. 'Gosh, it's cold today, isn't it?'

Joanne nodded. She'd worn her warm coat with gloves and a scarf but the cold nipped at her ears and nose, at her chin and lips, making her skin tingle. It was a beautiful Saturday and she was happy she'd booked it off from her job at the café, because it had meant that she'd got to come Christmas shopping with her friends.

'It feels like weeks since we had lunch and bought the pregnancy tests, doesn't it?' she asked.

'Hmmm.' Lila pulled her scarf up over her chin. 'It's only been four days but it feels like ages.'

'And you're OK about it all now, are you Lila?' Roxie rubbed Lila's back.

'Fine.' Lila gave them a small smile.

'It's OK if you're not OK, you know?' Roxie was peering at Lila, concern filling her eyes.

'I'm OK.' Lila nodded. 'Look, it's our turn to order.'

They'd reached the front of the queue at the food stall, so Roxie ordered three hot chocolates and three crepes then they waited while they were prepared. When the woman serving handed them to Roxie, she passed a crepe and hot chocolate to Lila and the same to Joanne, then they walked over to one of the picnic benches and sat down. The Christmas market was still fairly quiet as they'd arrived early, but Joanne suspected it would get busier as the day wore on.

They ate their crepes and drank their hot chocolate in silence, looking around at the other stalls and at the people who wandered past with bags of purchases, rosy cheeks and pink noses. Carols played from speakers attached to stalls and somewhere in the market there was a jingling of bells, as if Santa had arrived to give a guest appearance before the big day.

'That was delicious.' Joanne licked her lips then wiped them with a festive napkin.

'It was. There's something special about eating in the open air, especially in the winter,' Roxie said. 'Lila, honey, what are you doing?'

Lila was rooting around in her bag seeming completely oblivious to her friends.

'Oh . . . I was just looking for this.'

She set a small parcel on the table. It was wrapped in silver foil paper with a tiny red Christmas tree print and a red ribbon tied around it.

'What's that?' Joanne asked. 'It looks very fancy.'

'It's for you two.' Lila smiled. 'Open it.'

Roxie met Joanne's eyes and Joanne shrugged.

'Shouldn't we keep it for Christmas?' Roxie picked up the parcel and turned it over in her hands.

'No, it's fine. Open it now.' Lila nodded. 'It won't wait until Christmas. Well, it will but I can't wait until then.'

'OK . . . thank you.' Roxie pushed the parcel across the table to Joanne.

'Go on, Joanne, you can open it.'

'Thanks.'

Joanne pulled at the ribbon and the bow came undone then she peeled away a piece of sticky tape and opened the paper. She frowned.

'What is this, Lila?'

'What does it look like?'

'Like lots of pregnancy tests.' Joanne spread them out on the wrapping paper. 'There are . . . ten of them here and they're not in the wrappers, so I'm guessing they're used.'

Lila was grinning and nodding.

'That's a lot of wee.' Joanne pulled a face, thinking about how many times Lila had peed on the tests and now they were on a table where people put food and drink.

'Joanne, that's not the point.' Lila shook her head. 'The point is—'

'Lila!' Roxie cut her off. 'Does . . . this . . . mean . . . you're . . . *pregnant*?' Roxie's voice rose higher with each word.

'Yes!' Lila clapped her hands. 'That first test I did was negative initially, but when I checked it again . . . after you'd gone, there was a second faint line on it. We Googled it and found out that it could be an evaporation line and not a positive test, so I didn't know for sure right away.'

'We?' Joanne asked.

'It's a long story, but basically, I'd stuffed the test in the bin. Later on, when Ethan was home, Willy went through the bin and dug the test out.'

'That bloody cat.' Roxie laughed. 'It's as if he knew.'

'It really is.' Lila was laughing too. 'He'd been out but he came back in and when he dropped the test into Ethan's lap I was horrified but then Ethan looked at it and said it was positive. He thought Willy had taken it from someone else's bin, but I had to explain everything to him then.'

'How did he take it?' Joanne asked.

'Really well. He was a bit surprised, but then so was I when I saw the test, and because Google said it could be an evaporation line, he insisted we get in the van and drive to the supermarket and buy more tests to check. I told him I had a spare one there but he said we should be certain and get more than one type of test. I did some more tests that evening before bed and then the next day, some of the two line ones and digital ones, and they all came up positive. It's early days but it seems that I am pregnant.'

Joanne looked at Lila, at her rosy cheeks, her eyes bright with happiness and excitement and it made her throat ache with emotion.

'This is wonderful news, Lila!' She got up and went to Lila and hugged her then Roxie did the same and the three of them laughed and cried as they embraced.

'Oooh! Get a room!' A voice from behind them made Joanne look up. A man was staring down at them, a crooked grin on his face.

'Very funny!' Joanne shook her head, dismissing the stranger.

'No need for that,' he said.

Roxie stood up and put her hands on her hips, glaring at the man. 'We've just had some good news and are celebrating so why don't you mind your own business and bugger off?'

He held up his hands and his eyes widened. 'Sorry! I was just joking.'

'Well go do it somewhere else.' Roxie waved a hand at him dismissively and he shook his head then walked away.

'That was a bit harsh, Roxie.' Lila dabbed at her eyes with a tissue.

'I've got no time for knobs like that.' Roxie picked up the mugs they'd had their hot chocolates in. 'Why do they always feel the need to comment on things that don't concern them?'

'No idea.' Joanne shook her head.

'I can see that you'll be a very protective aunty to this baby,' Lila said.

'You bet I will.' Roxie gave a sharp nod. 'Right, I'll take these to the stall then we can have a look around.'

'What're you going to do with all these tests?' Joanne asked.

'I'll recycle them when I get home.' Lila picked them up and folded the wrapping paper around them as gently as if she was putting a nappy on a baby. 'You know, I can't quite believe it. This pregnancy wasn't planned but it's something I've found that I really want. Ethan and I will be parents, as long as it all goes well.' She crossed her fingers. 'Joanne, I'll be a mum.'

'And you'll be a lovely mum to a very lucky baby.' Joanne hugged her petite friend as a wave of love swept over her. She wanted to protect Lila and her unborn baby. Lila would make a wonderful mum and she had so much love and talent to share. Lila was a very creative person and she ran her own online business selling things she'd made like crocheted animals and blankets. Joanne could just imagine the little cardigans and hats that Lila could make for the baby and her belly clenched with excitement at the thought of what the next year would be like.

'Thank you, Joanne. I don't know how I'd cope without you and Roxie. I mean, I know Freda will be amazing when we tell her, but not having my own mum around can be difficult, especially at times like these.'

'Your own mum is a fool for not wanting to be around you, Lila, but you are right, you do have Roxie and me and we're always here for you. And as for Freda, she'll be a wonderful granny. I bet Ethan can't wait to tell her.'

'She will, I know. And your friendship means the world to me.'

'It does to me too. Now come on, let's get some Christmas shopping done. I'm sure I saw Roxie checking out some tree decorations at one of the stalls and it'll be funny if she takes more home because Fletcher will go mad.'

'He said that she's got enough to decorate Buckingham Palace already.'

'And then some!'

They linked arms and caught up with Roxie then they set off around the market, three women enjoying a day of Christmas shopping with their very best friends.

'Thanks for that. It was delicious.'

Max had made Joanne dinner, telling her that after a day of shopping it would do her good to relax. He'd made them Pasta Norma, based on the classic Sicilian dish that contained aubergines and tomatoes, and added a large green side salad and garlic bread.

'There's homemade chocolate mousse for dessert,' he said, as he got up to take the plates to the kitchen. They'd eaten on his large comfortable sofa, plates on their laps and feet on the coffee table with large glasses of a soft fruity red wine to wash the food down.

'You are amazing, Max! How did I get so lucky?'

'I'm the lucky one.' He winked at her.

'I'll do the dishes.'

'No you won't. You're my guest so you stay there and pour more wine and I'll pop these in the dishwasher then get the mousse.'

Joanne smiled at him, feeling thoroughly spoiled and relaxed. She was tired out after a day of Christmas shopping but also felt happy and satisfied in the way that she always felt after a day with Roxie and Lila. Both she and Roxie had been constantly aware of Lila's condition, asking her if she wanted to sit down or have a drink, and in the end, Lila had laughed and told them to stop fussing. She'd said she was pregnant, not ill, and promised to tell them if she felt at all tired or in need of anything.

When Max returned to the lounge, they scanned through the TV guide to find something to watch then settled back with their dessert. The mousse was rich, creamy and incredibly moreish. Joanne had discovered over recent weeks that Max was a skilled cook and that he also liked to spend time preparing meals, seeming especially happy when she enjoyed them — which she did every time.

'You are so talented,' she said after she'd licked her spoon clean.

'I like cooking for you. It's much better than just preparing food for myself. Cooking for one often seems like too much effort and I tended to settle for beans on toast or a baked potato with tuna mayo.'

He set their ramekins on the table then passed her a glass of wine.

'I found something out today.'

'Not that Santa isn't real?' Max grimaced and placed a hand to his chest. 'Please tell me it's not true!'

'Max!' She giggled. 'No, not that but for goodness sake keep your mouth shut about that around my niece and nephew.'

'Of course. Anyway, as far as I'm concerned Santa is real and anyone who says anything different is a fool.'

'Really?' She smiled at him, admiring how gorgeous he looked even in just a T-shirt and baggy jogging bottoms. It filled her with an urge to grab hold of him and kiss him hard.

'Really. Everyone needs to suspend their disbelief, especially about good things like Santa. It's all part of the Christmas magic. So don't worry, I'll make sure that your niece and nephew know that I'm a believer in the old man with the big white beard and the sleigh pulled by reindeer.'

Joanne reached out and stroked his cheek, feeling the brush of stubble against her skin, the curve of his jaw against her palm.

'I love you.'

His eyes widened slightly.

'I mean . . . I love being with you.'

He covered her hand with his, pressing it to his cheek. Something passed over his face and her heart sank as she wondered if she'd done the wrong thing telling him how she felt but it had just slipped out.

'Max, I'm so sorry. Please don't let that ruin anything. I didn't mean it like it sounded. It was just—'

'Joanne . . . I love you too.'

'You do?'

'Of course I do. I've been in love with you since our first kiss but I didn't know when to tell you. I was worried that I might scare you away.'

'You could never scare me away.'

'Was that what you found out today? That you love me?'

'What?'

'You said you found something out today.'

'Oh . . . no. It wasn't that. But it made me think about us and our relationship.'

'What was it?'

It's a secret so you mustn't tell anyone.'

'I promise.'

'I feel torn in a way and that perhaps I shouldn't tell you. But I also want to tell you because, well, I know you won't say anything.'

'You can trust me.'

'I know.' She nodded. 'Lila's pregnant.'

'Wow!'

He raised his eyebrows and Joanne faltered for a moment.

'I didn't mean that it made me think about us having children. Not at all. Just that it made me think about us and where we're headed and . . . things like that.'

He smiled. 'Do you want children?'

'Me?' she squeaked. 'I . . . I've never really given it a lot of thought because I'm quite traditional in the sense that I wanted, if I ever did get pregnant, to be in a relationship, and before you . . . there was nothing serious.' She sighed. 'Now I'm babbling.'

'You're beautiful.'

'You're so nice to me.'

'Joanne,' he placed their wine glasses on the table then took her hand and kissed the palm before running tiny kisses up her arm. She shivered with delight and her heart raced with longing. 'I love you and you love me. This is getting serious, isn't it?'

She slid her arms around his neck and gazed into his dark eyes.

'Yes.'

'I was wondering, actually . . . you were going to look for a house after Christmas anyway, but . . . how do you feel about moving in here? Or . . . if you don't like that idea, then we could look for somewhere together.'

'You want me to move in with you?'

'I don't want to spend another night apart from you.'

Joanne kissed him slowly, enjoying the feel of his lips against hers, his breath on her skin, his strong body against her.

When they finally broke apart, she held his gaze.

'Are you sure, Max?'

'I've never been more certain about anything.'

'Then yes, I'd love to move in with you.'

'Before Christmas or after?'

'Before will be a bit of a rush.'

'In the new year then?'

'That sounds good to me and it gives me some time to speak to Mum and Dad about it too. They do love you but you know how they worry.'

'Your parents are great.'

She kissed him again, excitement filling her as something she hadn't even allowed herself to think about was going to happen.

Perhaps this would be the Christmas when her wishes came true.

5

ROXIE

'Fletcher, where's Glenda's coat?'

'In the cupboard under the stairs?'

'Nope.'

Roxie went to the kitchen and checked in the dresser, but it wasn't there either. Glenda was following her around, a tiny shadow that kept bumping into her heels every time she stopped.

'You can't go out without your coat, Glenda. It's freezing this evening and you'll turn into a tiny block of ice.'

Fletcher appeared in the doorway holding Glenda's coat, a big smile on his handsome face.

'Found it. Come here, Glenda and let Dad put your coat on.'

Glenda raced across the kitchen, skidding on the tiles as she reached Fletcher. Roxie shook her head. 'You two!'

'I must've carried it up with me after walking her this morning,' Fletcher explained.

'It doesn't matter. You've found it now so we can get going. I don't want to miss the turning on of the lights.'

Fletcher clipped Glenda's harness on over the coat and they were ready to go.

Roxie pulled her faux fur hat on then stuffed her hands into her leather gloves. 'Do you think I'll be warm enough?' she asked as she peered at her reflection in the hall mirror. She was wearing a white and silver ski jacket with her hat and gloves, a soft grey scarf and knee-high boots.

'I'll keep you warm if you're not. But yes, I think you should be fine, and you look hot. Kind of like a French ski instructor.'

'That's your thing is it?'

'My wife is my thing and I have eyes for no one else.' He grabbed her and kissed her, taking her breath away. 'We'd better go or I'll have to keep you all to myself this evening.'

'Later, darling.' She winked at him. 'Ready, Glenda?'

They let themselves out of the house and made their way to the village green.

Fletcher held Glenda's lead with one hand and Roxie's in the other. He had always done this and she had always appreciated it. Even after all the years they'd been together, Fletcher was still considerate and caring, loving and romantic. They'd had their low moments, their bumps in the road — like in the summer when she'd suspected him of having an affair that he'd been completely innocent of — but they always came out the other side and Roxie knew that she would be lost without him. Fletcher was her best friend, her love and her rock and she adored him.

When they reached the green, people were milling around holding paper cups of mulled wine, cider and hot chocolate and mince pies or cartons of steaming chips. The air was fragrant with spices and salty chips doused with vinegar and Roxie's mouth watered.

'What do you want to drink?' Fletcher asked as he handed her Glenda's lead.

'Wine, please.'

'I don't know why I ask. You always want the mulled wine.' Fletcher gave her a quick kiss then headed for the drinks stand that was run by the village committee every year.

'See anyone you know, Glenda?' Roxie asked as they looked around. The small pug moved her head from side to side, taking everything in.

Fletcher returned with two cups of wine and handed one to Roxie. She took it carefully in case the wine was hot. Aromas of citrus and spice met her nostrils, instantly making her feel incredibly festive. The wine was warm and fragrant, cinnamon, cloves and nutmeg providing a gentle heat to the fruity beverage that made her lips and tongue tingle.

'Delicious as always,' she said and Fletcher nodded.

'It's very good.'

'I love this time of year.' Roxie's heart fluttered and she swallowed a bubble of emotion that took her by surprise. They'd come here to do this so many times and it was comforting, familiar and wonderful. Wisteria Hollow was a beautiful place to live and Roxie never took the scenery or the people for granted.

'Ah look, there's Joanne and Lila.' Roxie waved and her friends came over to her.

'Good evening,' Joanne said. 'You look like you're going skiing, Roxie.'

'Do I?' Roxie looked down at herself. 'That's what Fletcher said. Mind you, it would be nice, wouldn't it, Fletcher? A week on the slopes. But it would mean leaving our baby girl and I don't know about that.'

She looked down at Glenda and the pug looked up at her, one big tooth sticking out from under her top lip.

'You can take dogs on some holidays,' Lila said. 'And if not, I'm sure one of us could help.'

'You have her stay with you and those cats? Cleo would be fine, I'm sure, but not Willy. Glenda's terrified of him.' Roxie shuddered as she thought about how Glenda reacted whenever she saw the large black and white cat.

'That's true.' Lila nodded. 'Sorry.'

'I might be able to help.' Joanne smiled. 'I'm sure Mum and Dad wouldn't mind, but if it's after Christmas, Max and I could have her over.'

Roxie raised her cup of wine to her lips then paused as Joanne's words sank in.

'Excuse me?' She tilted her head on one side.

'Don't say anything, because I haven't told Mum and Dad yet but yes . . . Max asked me to move in with him.'

'That's brilliant!' Lila and Roxie said simultaneously, leaning in for careful hugs because they were all holding drinks.

'I know. I can't believe it.' Joanne grinned.

Roxie admired the blush in Joanne's cheeks (that she now knew was to do with more than the cold air) and the glimmer in her eyes and knew she was looking at one very happy friend.

'It's brilliant news. Will you move into his place or buy new, because we know you were saving for a deposit anyway?'

'I'm not sure yet but we'll talk about it over Christmas then make a decision.'

'Excuse me for a moment, Joanne.' Fletcher placed a hand on Roxie's arm. 'Roxie, I'm just going to go and say hello to a few people and leave you ladies to talk in peace.'

'Thanks, love.' Roxie gave him a quick kiss. She knew Lila and Joanne were aware that she shared most things with her husband, but he was being considerate by giving them some space to talk without feeling self-conscious.

'How did he ask you?' Lila asked, taking a sip of hot chocolate.

'We were talking and kissing and I told him I loved him and he said that he loves me back and then said he doesn't want to spend another night apart from me.'

'Awwwww!' Lila's smile lit her face up. 'That's lovely.'

'I'm so happy for you.' Roxie smiled and squeezed Joanne's free hand. 'So that's one friend pregnant and another moving in with her lover and that just leaves us in need of a wedding.'

'What?'

Roxie turned to find Ethan standing next to her frowning.

'Sorry, Roxie, did you just say one of your friends is getting married?' he asked.

Glenda bounced around with excitement. She'd got to know Ethan when he'd done some work at Roxie's and he was a firm favourite of hers. He crouched down to greet her and she tried to lick his chin.

'Hi Ethan.' Roxie smiled as he stood up again. 'No, what I said was that . . .' She felt Joanne and Lila's eyes boring into her. 'It's . . . uh . . . always nice to have a wedding in the village.'

'Oh.' He nodded then tugged the beanie he was wearing down over his ears. 'Right. Thought I heard differently then. You OK, Lila?' He wrapped an arm around her shoulders.

'I'm fine thanks, Ethan.' Lila gazed up at her boyfriend, her eyes filled with love.

'You look like you should be on the cover of one of those romcom Christmas movies,' Roxie said. 'All you need is a small dog.'

Glenda barked and they all laughed.

'You can borrow this one if you want.' She drained her wine and dropped the cup into a bin then scooped Glenda up and kissed her soft head. 'I don't mean it, Glenda. You know Mummy wouldn't part with you.'

'Uh . . . Roxie?' Ethan's eyes were wide as he looked at her.

'Yes?'

'I'll come over tomorrow and check that job out that you mentioned.'

'Job?' She frowned, wondering what job he was talking about.

'Yes you know . . . the paint job you want done. Wasn't it the downstairs toilet?'

'Was it?'

His eyes were holding hers, unblinking, and he was nodding, his mouth pulled into a tight smile. Roxie was aware of Lila and Joanne gazing curiously at them.

'Oh! Yes . . . of course. Sorry, Ethan. Silly me. *That* job. I'll be there all day so come over when you're free.'

'Brilliant.' He gave her a small wink, confirming her suspicion that he had something he wanted to talk to her about because she was quite certain she hadn't asked him to do any more jobs before Christmas. 'Looks like they're about to turn on the lights,' Ethan pointed over at the Christmas tree that stood tall and proud at the centre of the green.

'I love this part,' Joanne said, looking around.

'Are you looking for Max?' Roxie asked.

'Yes. Is it awful of me to want to be with him for this?'

'Of course not.' Roxie pointed across the green. 'He's over there with Fletcher. You coming too, Lila and Ethan?'

'Sure.'

They made their way over to Fletcher and Max and Roxie stood next to her husband, smiling as he slid an arm around her waist and held her close.

Then the countdown began.

'FIVE! FOUR! THREE! TWO! ONE!'

There was a collective gasp as the green was lit up with thousands of fairy lights. They were draped around the Christmas tree, around lampposts and fences and it seemed to Roxie as if the village had been scattered with tiny stars. It made the evening seem darker beyond the lights and her breath emerged in puffs that made her think of dragons in fairy tales. The air was glacial, the sky velvet black and the village picture perfect in its festive décor.

Music filled the air as the village choir began to sing 'White Christmas' and Roxie hugged Glenda closer while her husband did the same to her. She felt so lucky to have such a wonderful husband, beautiful little dog and lovely friends. Earlier in the year, she'd wondered how this year would end, but right now, it was looking like Christmas would be very merry indeed.

❋

*T*he next day, Roxie walked Glenda early, got home, showered and dressed then made some breakfast for her and Fletcher. She kept an eye on her phone, wondering if Ethan would text with a time but so far, she'd heard nothing. She'd asked Fletcher about it on the way home after the turning on of the lights but he'd been as much in the dark as she was.

The door finally went after 10 a.m., and Roxie answered it with Glenda, smiling as the dog jumped all over Ethan when he knelt down to say hello to her.

'Good morning. Want a coffee?'

'Please.' He nodded then followed her through to the kitchen, Glenda now in his arms. 'And thanks for last night.'

'No problem. I have to admit that I'm curious but I'm guessing it's something nice for Lila, so I'm all ears.'

'Glenda!' Ethan was laughing as the dog washed his chin, his cheeks and then tried to reach his ears.

'The good old ear snog, eh?' Fletcher entered the kitchen, freshly showered and smelling of shower gel and aftershave. Roxie breathed him in as he passed her, his scent so good that she could bury her face in him and stay there all day.

Ethan set Glenda down gently, still laughing. 'I've never had so much attention.'

'She does love her uncle Ethan,' Roxie said as she handed him a wet wipe to clean his face.

'Thanks.' He ran it over his skin then put it in the bin.

'There you go.' Roxie placed a mug in front of him then climbed onto a kitchen stool at the breakfast bar and Ethan sat opposite her.

'Would you like me to make myself scarce?' Fletcher asked as he picked up his own mug.

'No!' Ethan shook his head. 'I'd like to speak to both of you.'

Fletcher nodded then sat next to Roxie.

'What can we help you with then Ethan?' Roxie asked.

'You know about Lila, right?'

Roxie paused, wondering if he meant the pregnancy.

'That we're expecting?' he asked.

Roxie nodded. 'Yes. And congratulations. I meant to say as much last night but then you asked about the other thing and I got a bit flustered.'

'The other thing?'

'I'd mentioned that we needed a wedding on Sunflower Street because we already had one couple moving in together and a baby on the way.'

'Of course. Yes.' He nodded, his cheeks flushing. 'I thought I'd slipped up or something.'

'About what?' Roxie frowned. 'The baby?'

'No. See, the pregnancy wasn't planned but that doesn't mean the baby's not wanted. I mean . . . I'd kind of started to think about all this stuff as Lila and I became close and we're basically living together anyway, so I hoped there would be a next step. I guess I thought we might move in and get married first, but it doesn't matter at all. This pregnancy is very early on but it's delighted me to be honest. It feels right and that's all that matters.' He pushed a hand through his hair. 'However, regarding the other thing, the wedding, I was planning on asking Lila to marry me at Christmas. I've already got the ring and was going to propose over champagne on Christmas morning, but now, I want to make it even more special.'

'That's wonderful news! And you want some help?' Roxie asked.

'If you wouldn't mind. I want her to know how much I love her and to understand that this isn't just because of the baby. It's because she's come to mean the world to me.'

Roxie nodded but she couldn't speak. Her vision had blurred and her throat tightened and she could only move her head up and down and blink rapidly

'You OK, Roxie?' Fletcher touched her arm.

'I'm just . . . so happy for you both,' she finally squeaked.

'The thing is,' Ethan licked his lips, 'I know that this will be a big deal for Lila after what happened before. I don't want her to feel under any stress or to have any worries that I would ever hurt her the way that . . . that Ben did. She deserves to be happy and I'll do whatever I can to help with that.'

'Will she want a big wedding do you think?' Fletcher asked.

'I don't know.' Ethan wrapped his hands around his mug. 'I don't mind either way. I just want to make Lila happy.'

'She is happy, Ethan, and while she doesn't need a ring or a wedding to prove that you love her, I'm sure she will be delighted to be asked. I'm certain she'll say yes because she adores you.' Roxie dabbed at her eyes with a tissue.

'It's not easy for either of us. As you know . . . I was married before . . . and I never thought I'd fall in love again after I lost Tilly, but Lila has brought me back to life. She has saved me and I want to spend the rest of my days with her.'

'Stop it!' Roxie waved a hand and sniffed. 'You'll set me off again. In all honesty, I think you should propose then talk to her about what she wants afterwards. A quiet wedding with just a few friends and family members can be very special. That might well be what Lila wants with her not being close to her parents.'

'That's what I was thinking.' Ethan nodded. 'Less pressure and less expense, which is another bonus with a baby on the way.' He was worrying his bottom lip but his eyes were filled with joy. Roxie could see that he'd be a good husband and father. Lila had found her partner for life and he was a good one.

'Shall we have another coffee while we chat about some proposal ideas?' Roxie asked as she got off the stool and filled the kettle.

'Sounds good to me.' Ethan nodded. 'Fletcher's proposal in the summer, when he asked you to renew your vows, gave me a few ideas about how I could do this, actually. Thank you both so much.'

'No problem at all. But I think we should consider including Joanne too because she'll want to help.' Roxie knew Joanne would be devastated if she was left out of this surprise.

'Of course.' Ethan pulled his phone from his pocket. 'I have her number, so I'll send her a text and find out when she's available to help.'

Roxie glanced at Fletcher and his big grin made her smile too. They intended on renewing their vows after Christmas, so it seemed like the new year was going to be a very busy one indeed.

6

JOANNE

'You're going to have a Christmas party just so Ethan can propose to Lila?' Joanne asked Roxie as they strolled around the party shop.

Roxie shivered. 'These factory outlet places can be quite cold, can't they? And my answer to your question is yes and no. Fletcher and I love hosting you all and we thought that it would give Ethan a nice occasion to propose.'

'It is a lovely idea, Roxie. I just wanted to know if you were doing it all for Ethan and Lila because it's very generous of you.'

'I'll do anything for my friends, Joanne. You know that. And when Max decides that he wants to propose to you, or when you decide you want to propose to him, Fletcher and I will do what we can to help then too.'

Joanne laughed. 'I don't think we're quite there yet.'

'Yet!' Roxie wiggled her eyebrows. 'Exactly. But you will be.'

'I'm not sure, Roxie, I don't want to rush anything. Max is wonderful but we're talking about moving in together now, so I don't want to jump the gun.'

'Perhaps next year it'll be you two.'

Joanne smiled, knowing that Roxie could be right. Life could change in an instant and she knew that very well. One day she was single and in a lot of debt, the next she had cash to spare and a boyfriend. In part, the financial improvement back in the autumn had a lot to do with her mum and dad's generosity, as well as Roxie and Lila's help, but the boyfriend thing had been down to her and Max.

'Look at you smiling away, thinking about the man you love.' Roxie nudged her. 'Now . . . let's find everything silver that we can.'

'That's the theme?'

'Silver Christmas grotto. We'll set up a marquee again like we did for the Halloween party and decorate it with silver tinsel and lights and make it all romantic.'

'It sounds lovely.'

'It will be.'

'What about Lila though? She'll need some encouragement to get an appropriate outfit, won't she?'

'I hadn't thought of that! We need to take her clothes shopping and make sure that she has a gorgeous dress to wear. I'm thinking silver so it matches the theme, and we could get her to have ger hair done and wear a small tiara and—'

'It's a proposal not an actual wedding, Roxie.' Joanne could see that her friend was getting a bit carried away.

'Oops! You're right, Joanne. I just love a happy ending and want to see my friends happy and settled. I know it might be a bit old fashioned but when two people love each other, making a commitment is the perfect thing to do. I'm not saying that it has to be marriage or engagement, but a public commitment of some sort is lovely. And after what Lila went through with Ben the B, it's wonderful to see her so happy.'

'It is.' Joanne nodded. 'None of us know what's going to happen next, look at my sister as an example, but there's always a way to work things out.'

'There is. And for the times when the solution seems out of reach, there are friends to help you through.'

Joanne wrapped an arm around Roxie's shoulder. 'You're a softy, you know that?'

Roxie lifted her chin and sniffed. 'Now, now, Joanne, we'll have none of that nonsense.'

Joanne giggled, knowing Roxie was teasing her.

'Silver it is then!' Joanne started grabbing silver decorations off the shelves and dropping them into the trolley.

By the time they got to the counter, the trolley was full. They had tinsel, streamers, icicle lights, fairy lights and silver bunting. Joanne was excited by the idea of creating the grotto for the party and couldn't wait to tell Max about it.

They pushed the trolley out into the bright frosty morning then loaded it all into Roxie's car boot. The cold air swirled around their legs and whipped Joanne's hair up around her face making her think it resembled ginger candyfloss. She pushed it back behind her ears, shivering with pleasure as a memory of Max doing just that as they kissed in bed that morning popped into her head.

'It's freezing, isn't it?'

'It's going to get colder.' Roxie grimaced. 'One of the coldest Decembers on record apparently.'

'Have they forecast snow?'

'It's certainly a possibility.' Roxie gathered her coat tight over her chest. 'But, it would make the party even better wouldn't it? And that reminds me . . . I need to get Fletcher to order some patio heaters for the garden and marquee.'

'Do you want a hand with the food?'

Roxie smiled. 'No need, darling, I've already been in touch with a catering friend and they're happy to do the twenty-third.'

'Wonderful.'

'All we need to do now is stock up on wine and champagne.'

'Will it involve tasting?'

Roxie frowned then pulled her phone from her pocket. 'I'll tell Fletcher to get ready and that we'll pop the decorations back then he can drive us to get the booze. That way, you and I get to try before we buy.'

Joanne laughed. 'I was only joking. It's not even lunch time yet, Roxie.'

Roxie shrugged. 'You're not working today and I'm party planning. It won't hurt to have a few small glasses of something to warm us up. Besides which, it'll be gone noon by the time we get this stuff back and unloaded so it'll be fine.'

'You've twisted my arm.'

Joanne went around to the passenger side of the car and opened the door. Before getting inside, she took one more look at the bright blue sky. It didn't seem like there would be any snow today, but perhaps tomorrow or at the weekend, things would change.

The prospect of a white Christmas was very appealing indeed.

7

LILA

*L*ila was curled up in the corner of the sofa with Cleo warming her feet. The log burner was lit, Willy was lying in front of it, and the room was filled with a cosy glow. Outside, the afternoon was bright and cold, the wind whipping the clouds across the sky, and she was glad to be indoors with her cats. Ethan was working so the cottage was quiet but it no longer felt empty as it had done before he'd come into her life.

On her lap lay a ball of soft white wool and a crochet hook. She'd crocheted a lot lately, making toy greyhounds and other animals for her online shop, and recently she'd made some snowmen and women, reindeer and tiny Christmas trees. They'd sold quickly and people had contacted her to ask for more. Christmas was good for business and she aimed to make more festive stock next year to sell in the winter months. She'd need to make more money anyway if there was going to be another mouth to feed.

She pressed a hand to her belly and closed her eyes, trying to imagine what was going on inside her right now. The previous day, she'd been to the doctor and had a pregnancy test there. It had confirmed that she was expecting, and she'd felt a flip of excitement when the GP had told her the result Everything suddenly seemed real, official, and it was sinking in that as long as all went well, she'd have a baby in around eight months' time. The GP had said that according to Lila's dates, she was about four to five weeks pregnant, then checked her blood pressure and talked her through what to expect over the next few weeks, as well as what to eat and drink to ensure that she and the baby were as healthy as possible.

Lila had popped to the supermarket after her GP appointment and picked up some pregnancy magazines. The glossy mags showed images of women with rounded tummies and rosy cheeks, glossy hair and bright eyes. Lila's own stomach was still flat and smooth, but she knew that it would change and wasn't sure yet how she felt about that. Growing a baby was a huge responsibility and it came with a whole new set of anxieties. Could she do this? Could she get the baby safely through the next eight months? Could she be a good mother, knowing how her own mother had been or would she be tainted by her past? Was she equipped to be a good mum? Was Ethan really ready for this? He'd been through so much in the past and was such a lovely man but was he ready to be a dad?

She ran a hand over the ball of wool, feeling it soothe her. Being creative had always comforted her, taken her mind off her worries and this didn't have to be any different. Worrying was natural, surely, but women got through pregnancies and births every day and they did fine. Why shouldn't she? It was true that her parents hadn't wanted her, then Ben hadn't wanted her, but it didn't mean that she was worthless, just that they were the wrong people for her. Lila's friendship with Roxie and Joanne had taught her that, her growth as an adult woman had taught her that, and her time with Ethan had confirmed it all. Lila was a warm, caring human being and she deserved to be respected and loved. She was strong and she could do this and not screw it up in the way her parents had done.

Before Ben had left her, she'd dreamt about the babies they would have. They'd bought the cottage using some of Lila's inheritance from her grandmother as a deposit, and Lila had pictured herself bringing babies home, rocking them to sleep in front of the fire, marking their growth on the kitchen wall, baking cakes with them and walking them to school. Her dreams had been simple ones but wanting a family of her own had been, in part, her way of trying to make up for her childhood and she'd craved security and love. For a while, Ben had seemed to provide a form of love and they'd been together for seven years, but not all of that time had been happy, not all of it had been nice. There had been good times and she knew that Ben had a positive side, but his dissatisfaction with their relationship had made him unhappy and then he'd taken that out on her. With hindsight, she could look back and see the cracks in their relationship, trace the lines that widened into crevices and canyons, whereas back then, she'd just tried harder to be what he wanted her to be. She had been deliberately blind because she'd wanted everything to be fine. It would never have worked long term because a person had to be true to their heart and she knew that now.

Ben leaving had broken her for a while but also taught her valuable lessons about herself, then she had met Ethan and her life had changed again, and so she could never hate Ben. He had done what he needed to do at the time and though he could have been kinder in how he ended their relationship, left before she'd planned the wedding and reached their wedding day, ultimately he had set Lila free from what would have been a difficult marriage.

Lila's life had changed beyond recognition in just under two years. If someone had told her as she sobbed on her wedding day that she'd meet someone else and get pregnant by him, she'd never have believed it and yet it was true. She breathed in slowly, sending love and positivity through her body to the tiny being just beginning in her womb, hoping that all would be well and that she would meet her child the following summer. An August baby would be wonderful and this time next year, Christmas could be magical, her best Christmas yet.

She picked up the crochet hook and loosened the end of the wool then made a loop. It was very early to make anything for the baby in her belly, but that didn't mean she couldn't make baby clothes and baby blankets to sell in her online shop. If she happened to keep one or two of them as the months wore on, then that would be all right too, because she would feel more secure once she'd passed the twelve-week mark. It seemed like an age away right now and that was scary, but it would also give her time to adapt, to practise self-care and to prepare for the new arrival. There would be a baby on Sunflower Street next year and it was something to look forward to.

8

ROXIE

'I adore Covent Garden,' Lila said.

'Me too. Especially at Christmas.' Roxie was glad she'd suggested the trip, even if it was under the guise of Christmas shopping. Really, it was to get Lila a dress for the party, but they could also pick up some gifts and soak up the festive cheer.

They'd caught the train from Wisteria Hollow and headed straight for Covent Garden, aiming to make the most of their day out.

'Where first?' Joanne asked.

'How about we mosey around and see what takes our fancy?' Roxie suggested, giving Joanne a sly wink when Lila was looking in the other direction.

'Lovely.' Joanne nodded, returning the wink.

The morning was grey and bitterly cold, but Roxie didn't mind because it was proper wintery weather and Covent

Garden was particularly festive. The 60-foot Christmas tree and the thousands of lights around the historic piazza and surrounding streets were magical, and the three of them stood and admired the tree and lights for some time, each one lost in their thoughts about the year just gone and the new one to come.

'I read that there are over 30,000 lights on the tree and 115,000 around the district,' Joanne said as she turned around, peering upwards.

'That's a big electricity bill.' Lila giggled. 'Can you imagine?'

'It's incredible though.' Roxie gazed at the tree that stood like a giant overlooking the piazza. She could imagine that it was guarding the area, keeping an eye on the people who scurried around carrying bags and shopping lists, thinking of what to buy for friends and loved ones and wondering if the turkey they'd ordered would be big enough to feed everyone.

Lila shivered and Roxie touched her arm. 'You OK, sweetie?'

'I just had the realisation that there will be a baby here this time next year. Not *right* here, but possibly with us, or at home with Ethan. If all goes well that is. I keep having little wobbles at the moment when the shock of being pregnant hits me again and again.'

'It will keep happening for a while yet, I'm sure.' Roxie smiled. 'Just try to stay calm and accept it. Everything will be fine.'

Lila's eyes widened. 'I hope so, Rox, and yet I think I'm just a bit afraid to hope. What if I let myself love this baby then something goes wrong?'

Roxie swallowed and took a deep breath. 'Nothing comes without risk, Lila, but I have a very good feeling that this baby is healthy and strong and will arrive next summer. I do know how difficult it is to escape the fear . . . but you're young and strong and you'll be fine.'

Lila nodded, gratitude filling her eyes. Roxie did know, of course, how wonderful it could be to be pregnant, but she also knew how dreadful it was when things didn't work out. Losing her own twins had broken her and it had taken her a long time to heal, but she had come through it and so had Fletcher. They'd been devastated and had never got over it, more learned to live with it. What else could they do? They had suffered a huge loss but they had each other and so they had clung together and emerged stronger than before, more devoted than before, filled with belief that they were meant to be. And, although she had lost her babies, it didn't mean that she couldn't be happy for Lila and delighted for her. Lila would be a wonderful mum and Roxie was excited about seeing her with her child.

They wandered around, admiring the other, smaller Christmas trees, each one adorned with a unique set of decorations. Inside the market building there were giant mistletoe chandeliers and everywhere they looked outside, lights twinkled and decorations created a wonderful festive feel.

'Ooh, look! There's going to be a wreath making workshop.' Lila pointed at a sign.

'It's not until this evening though.' Roxie checked her watch. 'It's not even eleven o'clock yet.'

'We might still be here then if we have a busy day and we could stay for the workshop, couldn't we?' Lila grinned at

her, hands clenched as if in prayer, and Roxie saw the child
Lila would have been: petite, blonde, sweet and innocent.
Excited about life. Neglected by the two people who should
have adored her, loved her, nurtured her.

'What do you think, Jo?' Roxie raised her eyebrows. 'Our
creative friend here would like to stay and take a class in
wreath making.'

'I'm game.' Joanne nodded. 'As long as you feed me regularly to keep my blood sugar even.'

'Wonderful. That's settled then.' Roxie got her phone out of
her bag. 'I'll just let Fletcher know so he can help himself to
dinner and not wait for me.'

'Is that gingerbread?' Joanne pointed at a small portable stall
where people were queuing. Steam rose into the air from a
small chimney in the roof and the stall itself looked like a
gingerbread house out of a picture book.

'I think so.' Roxie got her purse out. 'Shall we go and refuel
before we hit the shops?'

'Yes please.' Lila and Joanne replied.

They joined the queue and Roxie's mouth watered as the
scent of ginger and other spices teased her nostrils. There was
nothing like warm gingerbread, fresh and soft on the inside,
its spices gently warming the mouth and tongue. The stall
also sold hot chocolate and Roxie realised she really wanted
one of those too.

When they'd been served, they carried their treats to a quiet
spot in front of a clothes boutique. Roxie bit into the gingerbread, savouring the flavours.

'This could be my morning sickness cure.' Lila held up her gingerbread. 'I could eat this every day to stave off those horrid waves of nausea I've read about.'

'Are you feeling nauseous then?' Roxie asked.

'No . . . but I've read that most pregnant women suffer from it to some degree or other so it's likely that I'll experience it.'

'I had it. Terrible it was. But then, it was a twin pregnancy so perhaps it was worse.' Roxie shrugged, remembering the awful feeling. 'Gingerbread would have helped though, I'm sure.'

Lila's bottom lip quivered and her eyes filled with tears.

'Lila! What's wrong?'

'I . . . I'm so sorry you lost your babies. It's so tragic.'

Roxie shook her head, unable to hug Lila because she had a hot chocolate in one hand brimming with whipped cream and marshmallows, and the rest of her gingerbread in the other. 'It's OK. I'm OK, honestly. I was just thinking about how awful morning sickness can be. Look . . . you don't have to worry about me. I'm delighted for you and can't wait to meet your little one. If I do agree with something you're going through based on my own experiences, you don't need to feel bad. I went thought that pregnancy and although I lost the babies, I'll never forget them. Thinking about them does make me sad sometimes but I also treasure the memory of them.'

'You're so brave.' Lila sniffed.

'We're all brave, sweetheart, and all fighting our own battles. I have the rose bushes in my garden and whenever I feel the need to talk to my babies, I go outside and sit with them. I know they're not physically there, but it makes me feel closer to them somehow because we bought the rose bushes with the twins in mind. There are lots of ways to find comfort after suffering a loss and that is one of mine. Now . . . drink your hot chocolate and then we can go and spend some money.'

'OK.' Lila managed a smile. 'Thank you.'

'Shall we go in there first.' Joanne gestured behind them at the boutique. 'I need a Christmas outfit.'

'It looks expensive.' Lila frowned. 'I doubt that they do maternity wear.'

'Lila, you're tiny and you won't be much bigger in two weeks, so I'm sure it'll be a while before you're in maternity clothes.'

'I guess so.' Lila looked down at her belly that was still flat in her indigo jeans.

'But you could buy a nice dress for our party.' Roxie's eyes had fallen on a silver gown in the window. It looked incredibly soft and silky and had capped sleeves and a layered skirt that fell to the mannequin's ankles. It would be perfect for Lila.

'Good idea.' Lila nodded. 'Even if I can't wear it for a while afterwards, I'd like to get something nice.'

'That's settled then.' Roxie drained her paper cup. 'Drink up and let's shop.'

*I*nside the boutique it was quiet and cool, the fragrance of lilies permeating the air. It was a contrast to the street outside where Christmas tunes played and people trudged around, where aromas of food and drink were strong and where life felt real and gritty. In the boutique, it was as if time had stood still and a moment had been captured and frozen.

Lila and Joanne seemed to move closer to Roxie as if afraid to stand too far away. She could smell the gingerbread and hot chocolate on them and wondered if they should have waited a while before coming inside. Everything looked shiny and clean, from the rows of white and silver garments to the polished shelves and gleaming counter complete with a till that looked like something out of a spaceship.

'Perhaps we should go somewhere else,' Lila whispered as she hunkered even closer to Roxie.

'Yes . . . I'm not sure about this shop at all.' Joanne gawked at the clothes around them.

'Don't be silly. We have just as much right as everyone else to be in here. Therefore, have a look at the clothes and see if you can find something for Christmas.'

Roxie sent her friends in opposite directions, suppressing a smile as they reminded her of ballet dancers in a performance of *Swan Lake* with their arms raised to avoid knocking anything off hangers and their slow graceful movements. They were clearly uncomfortable in the shop, but Roxie wanted them to feel that they belonged there just as much as anyone else. She couldn't abide snobbery and always made an effort to question it.

'Hello. Can I help you?'

A very tall, thin woman with her hair scraped back into a tight bun peered at Roxie from behind the counter. Had she been there when they'd come in? She was so thin that she could have been standing behind a mannequin and that would explain why they hadn't seen her.

'We're looking for some Christmas outfits.'

The woman's blonde eyebrows raised slightly but her forehead remained flat and line free. She gave Roxie a quick glance from head to toe that some might have missed but Roxie was observant.

'Christmas outfits, eh?' The woman came out from around the counter, her black fitted dress with a white panel at the front making Roxie think of a penguin. 'Would that be for dinner or a party?'

'A party.' Roxie inclined her head. 'A very important party.'

'Aha! How exciting.' Penguin tried to smile but it resulted in a strange quivering of her left eyebrow and a twitching of her upper lip. Too much Botox, Roxie suspected.

'I'd like a dress.' Lila had appeared at penguin's side.

Penguin shot round and gave Lila the onceover and clearly liked what she saw.

'Of course. And what about your friend?' She nodded at Joanne. 'Does she want something too?'

'Yes, please.'

'Let me show you to the changing room and I'll bring you a selection of garments.'

'But don't you need to know our sizes?' Lila asked, her brows meeting.

'I can take an educated guess.' Penguin gave what looked like a small bow then glided away.

Lila stepped closer to Roxie. 'It's not exactly bargain shopping in here, Rox.'

'I know but this is for a special occasion and besides which, they've got a pre-Christmas sale on.' She pointed at a tag on a coat. 'Up to 30% off.'

'That's something I guess although "up to" is the wording you have to be mindful of.'

'Ladies!' Penguin was waving them over. 'The changing rooms.'

'Better not keep her waiting,' Roxie muttered, and they hurried over, meeting Joanne on their way.

Inside the changing rooms was like a spacious igloo and Roxie gasped. The walls were flawless white with a round white velvet sofa at the centre. What seemed like chiffon drapes billowed from the ceiling around the edges, making Roxie think of a wedding tent. The scent of lilies was stronger and the air cooler and she shivered as if someone had stroked a finger down her spine.

'It's like a funeral parlour,' Joanne said, her voice seeming loud in the space.

'Don't, Joanne. It is a bit creepy though, isn't it?' Lila grimaced.

'You two are so dramatic. There I was thinking it seems like an igloo and the shop assistant is like a penguin.'

'A penguin?' Lila snorted.

'A skinny penguin.' Joanne shook her head 'And where are the changing cubicles? Or is it one of those communal ones?'

Roxie stared at the walls. 'I'm assuming they're behind the curtains though I can't make them out.'

'Ladies,' Penguin was back, 'I have some things here for you. I'll hang them on different rails so you don't get them mixed up.'

She pushed on the wall behind her and a door opened to what appeared to be a cupboard. She pulled out a hanging rail on wheels then hooked several garments over it. 'This is yours.' She gestured at Lila.

'Where do I change?'

Penguin turned back to the cupboard and pressed a button on what appeared to be a control panel then the walls around them moved and four spacious and well lit cubicles appeared behind the curtains.

'The designers thought this would save space and impress customers and while it does save space, it's not very impressive when the walls stick.' Penguin gave her head a small shake. 'You can just pull the curtains in front of each cubicle aside.'

'Thanks.' Lila pulled the rail behind her and went into the nearest cubicle and pulled the curtain across, although with it being chiffon, they could still see her.

'I'll just get your selections.' Penguin left the changing room and Roxie looked around.

'This has to be the strangest changing room I've ever seen.'

'It's like something out of a science fiction movie.' Joanne giggled. 'Let's hope those walls don't move back when we're inside the cubicles.'

Roxie shivered. 'Don't! I'm getting changed out here.'

When Penguin had delivered their clothes and hung them on rails, Roxie and Joanne took a look at what she'd brought. Roxie was impressed by the woman's estimate of her size and taste and started to undress so she could try them on.

Lila emerged from her cubicle and smiled shyly.

'What do you think?'

It was the silver dress from the window. It clung to her slim frame and as she turned from side to side the skirt swirled around her legs like a silken waterfall.

'That's the one,' Roxie said. 'I saw it in the window and knew it was perfect for you.'

'Is it though?'

'It really is.' Joanne nodded. 'Don't try anything else on because that is the perfect dress for a Christmas prop—'

'Joanne!' Roxie interrupted and Joanne's expression turned to one of horror. 'Joanne means it's perfect for a Christmas party.'

Lila appeared oblivious to Joanne's slip and was twirling around, arms extended as the dress floated around her. She was such a beautiful woman, so delicate and refined, and Roxie experienced a surge of love for her. How anyone could ever have hurt Lila she had no idea. It would be like kicking a puppy or abandoning a kitten. Lila's parents were missing out on so much. If Roxie had been lucky enough to have a daughter, she'd have loved her, cared for her and prioritised her happiness over everything else. Sometimes she failed to understand people at all and wondered why those who didn't want children sometimes had them and others who longed for children sometimes couldn't have them. There was a lot about life that was unfair.

She shook herself.

There was also a lot about life that was wonderful, and she strove to remember that. Her cup was full, and she had much to be thankful for.

'That's the one, Lila. Try the others on if you like but I don't think you'll find one prettier than that.'

Lila nodded then went back to the cubicle. 'I'll just change out of it then I can help you two decide on what you want.'

Half an hour later, they had paid and were back outside. The air had grown colder during their time in the boutique and the sky had darkened. It made the tiny lights seem brighter and the enormous Christmas tree all the more magnificent.

'What's next?' Lila asked.

'How about helping me find something for Glenda?' Roxie asked. 'She told me she wanted a new winter coat.'

'Told you?' Joanne cocked an eyebrow.

'She did.'

Roxie turned her back to the boutique then held out her arms. 'Shall we?'

Lila and Joanne hooked their arms through Roxie's then they set off around Covent Garden, savouring the aromas of spices, the twinkling lights and the cheerful carols that filled the air.

9

LILA

'*I* am exhausted.' Lila dropped her bags in the hallway and kicked off her shoes. 'That was such a busy day.'

Ethan had opened the door to her and now he closed it behind him then took her coat.

'You were out a long time.' He hung her coat under the stairs then opened his arms. 'I missed you.'

'I missed you too.' She walked into his embrace and sighed with contentment. It was lovely to have a day out with friends, but it was wonderful to come home to Ethan.

'Cup of tea?' he asked.

'Yes please.'

He released her then picked up her bags and carried them through to the kitchen. It was warm and cosy and smelt delicious. There was a pot bubbling on the top of the Aga and the aroma of garlic and something rich and savoury made her mouth water.

'What are you cooking?'

'Chicken chasseur. I haven't eaten yet because I thought you might be hungry when you got home. I've got steamed broccoli and buttered carrots to go with it and potatoes boiling for mash.'

'Yum! That all sounds amazing.'

'I have to look after my beautiful girlfriend and our precious baby.'

He set the bags down then came to her and placed a hand on her belly. 'I can't believe that there's a person in there.'

'I don't know that he or she resembles a person at the moment, more a tiny wonky bean, but I know what you mean.'

'We created a life together, Lila, and that's incredible.'

She nodded as emotion surged in her throat. Ethan was so happy about their unplanned pregnancy that she was beginning to feel like it was meant to happen. Yes, they could have waited a few years, and yes, it would have been nice to have planned it, but with each day that passed, the baby was wanted every bit as much as it would have been had it been planned.

'How long will dinner be?' she asked.

'About half an hour. There's time for you to have a bath if you want then you can get your pyjamas on and we can eat in front of the TV.'

'That sounds perfect.'

'What did you buy?' He looked at the bags.

'Lots.' She laughed. 'Including a rather fancy dress for Roxie's Christmas party.'

'She persuaded to get one, did she?' He smiled

'Want to have a look?'

'No!'

'Oh . . . OK.' She blinked. Why had he answered so sharply? 'I thought you'd like to see it that's all. I didn't mean to bore you with women's fashion.'

'It's not that. And you never bore me. I love seeing what you've bought, and you always look beautiful, but I thought it might be nice to wait until the party. Then it will be a surprise.'

Lila chewed her bottom lip. Was she being oversensitive here? It made sense to surprise him. After all, it was something that could help to keep a relationship fresh if they surprised each other from time to time. And the dress was pretty special so it would be nice for him to see it on her rather than on a hanger.

'OK.' She nodded. 'We can wait. It's the most expensive item I've ever bought . . . except for a wedding dress, that is, and I'd never spend that on a dress again . . . sorry, I know you don't want to hear about that. When I saw the price tag on this dress, I almost left it there, but Roxie and Joanne persuaded me to get it. They said it's perfect and it would be criminal of me not to buy it, so I did. I guess I just need to make about a hundred more crocheted greyhounds to pay for it.'

Ethan was gazing at her, his head tilted, an expression of curiosity on his face.

'What is it?' she asked, uncertainty filling her.

'You.'

'Me?'

'I love you, Lila. You're just . . . such a special person. You deserve beautiful dresses and I can't wait to see this one on you. And, seeing as how you mentioned the subject of your non wedding to Ben, can we agree that it is OK for you to talk about it? I really don't mind. You have a past. I have a past. We weren't teenagers when we met but it doesn't matter. We are where we are in life because of what we've been through. I was married, you were almost married. I lost Tilly to circumstances beyond our control. You lost Ben, or rather, I like to think of it as Ben lost you because he was an idiot and didn't appreciate what he had. However, his loss is my wonderful gain and I am so glad that we found each other. You have made me want to live again and now we have a baby on the way and a life together. I have so much more than I thought I would ever have after Tilly died.'

He caressed her face, placed his strong hands on her shoulders and held her gaze.

'I love you too, Ethan.'

He kissed her softly, wrapping his arms around her and she felt safe, loved, protected. And inside her, she knew that their baby was safe, loved and protected and that together they would be the loving parents their child deserved.

'I also made a festive wreath,' she said, when they broke apart.

'Let's have a look then.'

She reached for the paper bag and removed the wreath that she'd made earlier in the workshop. It consisted of leaves, flowers, evergreens and twigs that she'd twisted together to create a ring. She'd then fixed cinnamon sticks, dried oranges and pinecones to the wreath and it smelt wonderful.

'That's gorgeous. Shall we hang it on the front door?'

'That's what I was thinking.'

'Seems a shame to put it outside but then we'll see it every time we go out and come home so I guess that makes sense. I'll hang it when you're in the bath.'

'Cats OK?'

'Yes, they've eaten and Cleo's in front of the fire but I think Willy went out. Probably sulking because you weren't here.'

'My grumpy little boy.'

'You could have another one soon.'

'Don't! Can you imagine? What if we do have a grumpy baby?'

'How could it be grumpy with a mum like you?' He grinned and she giggled.

'I'm off for my bath.'

'Your dinner will be ready when you come down.'

She gave him a kiss then picked up the bags with her dress and his Christmas gifts inside and took them upstairs with her. Feeling so happy was something she valued immensely after what she'd been through and she still experienced the need to pinch herself to check she wasn't dreaming.

Life was so good right now and she wanted to hold on tight and keep it that way forever.

'The tree looks perfect,' Lila sat back on the sofa and admired the real tree that Ethan had picked up and decorated that afternoon while she'd been out.

'I'm glad you think so. Are the coloured lights OK?'

'Perfect.' She leant her head on his shoulder and gazed at the tree he'd placed in front of the window, adorned with tiny colourful lights. 'I adore the scent of pine and the fact that it can be planted out after Christmas.'

'We have to remember to water it every day.'

'I'm sure we will. And, Ethan, that was the best meal I've had in ages.'

'Really?'

'It was delicious. You are such a good cook. In fact, I think you should make all the meals from here on.'

He grinned. 'I will if you want.'

'I'm only teasing you. I'm happy to do my fair share but it is lovely to have some meals made for me.'

'As you get bigger and after the baby is born, I'll do more around here, I promise. I'm happy to cook more anyway but I'll certainly do more whenever you need more rest. Like, I think you should leave the ironing and washing to me as it is.'

'What? No way. That's not fair on you, Ethan. You go out to work every day.'

'You work from home. It's no different.'

'But I can pop a wash on when I'm here. It's no trouble.'

He took her plate from her and placed it on the table. 'I just don't want you wearing yourself out. You need to rest as much as possible.'

'I will, I promise.'

He took her hand. 'Can I get you some dessert?'

Lila shook her head. 'I'm stuffed, thanks. I ate my bodyweight in gingerbread today and drank the same in hot chocolate. I suspect Roxie will be running about ten miles tomorrow after the amount she put away too.'

'It's good that you all had a lovely time.'

'We did. I'm lucky to have such good friends.'

'They are good friends and have been very kind to me too. I feel accepted by them.'

'You are. They love you too.'

His cheeks flushed and he lowered his gaze to their hands.

'What is it?' she asked.

'I've just been thinking the past week or so . . . since we found out about you being pregnant, that life is strange sometimes.'

'In what way?'

'Well . . . your parents didn't treat you very well and my father didn't want to know about me. I can't imagine ever feeling that way about our child.'

'Nor me.'

'It's like . . . how can you have a child and not care about it? I can't wait to meet our baby and I'm going to love him or her and protect him or her with everything I am. I know you'll be the same. And yet . . . out there somewhere, my father is living a life not giving a damn and your parents are too. What is wrong with people?'

There was hurt and anger in his voice and Lila wanted to hold him close and soothe him. She raised her head and slid an arm around his shoulders then kissed his forehead.

'Sorry, I'm not being very manly, now am I?'

'Oh Ethan, please don't ever worry about that. And what is *manly* anyway? I don't want some machismo machine that doesn't care or feel. I want you and everything that comes with you. Believe me, it breaks my heart to think that your father doesn't care but sadly, it's one of those things. With me, I'll think I've come to terms with the estrangement from my parents and then it will creep up on me and hit me hard. Of course it will be the same for you. And, as you said, now that we have a child on the way, we're bound to think about our own parents more. I can't make sense of their behaviour either but all I do know is that I've learnt from it and I want to be a better mum than mine was. You will be a better dad too. That's all we can take away from it really. I think we'll always have a part of us that will be sad that our parents, except for your mum of course, don't care but we won't let it ruin our lives. We'll live with it and forgive them, because resentment will only eat away at us, and we'll wish them well. But we don't have to let their actions and attitudes affect us and our futures.'

Ethan nodded. When he raised his eyes she could see that they were shining.

'It's not easy but then I don't think any family relationships are.' Lila chewed at her bottom lip.

'Thank you for listening and for caring.'

'Never be afraid to tell me how you're feeling. We're a team now and we're here for each other so forget about manly and strong and all that. If we work together, there's nothing we can't deal with.'

He slid his arms under her and lifted her on to his lap then hugged her tight. With her head resting on his shoulder and their hearts beating as one, Lila felt a surge of love rush through her. Everything would be OK as long as they had each other.

10

JOANNE

'Right . . . I have something to tell you.' Joanne looked at her parents across the kitchen table the following Monday morning. After speaking to Max at the weekend, they'd decided she should tell her parents their plan to move in together so they had time to get used to the idea before the new year.

Her mum's pale eyebrows rose then she turned to her dad and he pulled the same face.

'Are you pregnant, Joanne?' Her dad asked as calmly as if he was asking what shift she was working tomorrow.

Joanne rubbed her face. 'No, Dad, I'm not pregnant.'

Her mum's eyebrows settled again. 'Shame.'

'What do you mean, "shame"?' Joanne asked.

'Well . . . when we saw you and Roxie last week, your dad spotted a pregnancy test in the basket and so we thought it might be for you. I mean . . . Roxie's a bit old to have a baby now, with her being almost fifty, and so we guessed it might be you. We were waiting for you to tell us but then you didn't so we thought the test must have been negative.'

'Mum, I'm not and have never been pregnant. I . . . don't want to be pregnant either.'

'But you and Max would have such beautiful babies together.'

Joanne sipped her tea, wishing it was wine, even thought it was still very early.

'That might be true, but we've only been together five minutes and are certainly not ready to have a child together.'

'But—'

'Mum! Please. Let that idea be for now.'

'I was just going to ask who the test was for if it wasn't for you.' Her mum's green eyes were wide and unblinking behind her glasses as she gazed at Joanne. She pushed a strand of her dyed ginger hair behind her ear and waited.

'Please, please don't say anything if I tell you.'

'We promise. Don't we, Rex?' Her mum nudged her husband.

'Yes, Hilda, we promise.' Her dad placed a hand over his heart as if demonstrating his integrity.

'It was for Lila.'

Her mum's mouth formed a perfect O and her dad nodded.

'Thought so,' her dad said, running a hand over his thick moustache.

'You did not, Rex. You were convinced it was for Joanne.'

He shrugged. 'And if not, then I thought it was for Lila, because as you said, Hilda, Roxie is a bit old to be having a baby.'

'Women can have babies at any age now, Mum and Dad.' Joanne shook her head. 'Anyway, that doesn't matter. What does matter is that you don't breathe a word to anyone. Lila wants it kept quiet for now because it's very early in the pregnancy.'

'Of course, Joanne. We'll keep quiet. But can I start knitting?' her mum asked. 'I do love knitting for a baby.'

'I know.' Joanne nodded. When her sister, Kerry, had been pregnant, her mum had knitted what seemed like hundreds of garments and blankets for the babies and in the end, Kerry had asked her to slow down because she was overrun with baby clothes.

'I'll dig out my patterns later and make a visit to the wool shop tomorrow.'

'Mum!' Joanne sighed. 'This is what I was talking about. You can't go telling anyone and I know what you're like. If you go to the wool shop and buy wool specifically for baby clothes, you'll slip up or someone will start asking questions that you'll struggle to answer.'

Her mum raised her chin and sniffed. 'I can be discrete, Joanne, and if people want to come to any conclusions at all then I'll let them think it's for you or Kerry.'

'Great. Thanks. That's just what I need right now.'

They fell silent around the table and Joanne drained her mug, then got up to make another.

'What was your news, Joanne?' her dad asked.

'Oh . . . I forgot about that. Mum's baby talk distracted me.'

She went back to the table and sat down, wishing she had a cup of tea to hold so she had something to do with her hands.

'I . . . Max and I . . . have decided to move in together after Christmas.'

The gasp that emerged from her mum made Joanne's heart thud. It sounded as though she was having a panic attack.

'Mum! Are you OK?'

'Yes.' Her mum nodded, her cheeks red and her mouth stretched into a grin. 'That is wonderful news.'

'Congratulations, Joanne.' Her dad got up and gave her a hug. 'He's a very pleasant young man.'

'Have you told your sister yet?' her mum asked.

'No. I wanted to tell you and dad first.'

'Ring her now! Let her know. She'll be so happy for you.'

'Hilda, Kerry will be at work right now.'

'But she'll want to know.'

'We can tell her later. Or, actually, Joanne can. It's her news.'

Her mum clapped her hands together and Joanne shifted in her seat. She'd hoped her parents would be happy for her, but this was far more than she'd expected.

'I want to tell someone.' Her mum was visibly bouncing on her chair now, her giant bosom heaving under her floral button front apron, and Joanne wondered what she'd started.

'Tell who you like, Mum. This isn't a secret.'

'I'm so happy.' Her mum got up and hugged Joanne then shuffled from the kitchen, leaving Joanne and her dad to pull faces at each other.

'You've made your mum's day then.'

'Looks that way. I suspect she's off to phone all her friends.'

'She'll be asking about the wedding soon, you know.'

Joanne rolled her eyes. 'Don't.'

'It's not even that she thinks you have to be married to live together, more that she wants you to be happy.'

'I didn't need a man to make me happy, Dad.'

'Your mum and I know that, but she'll be happy that there's someone else to love you and care for you. She's always worrying about what'll happen after we're gone and just wants to know that you, Kerry and the grandchildren are being looked after.'

'Mum has a heart of gold, doesn't she?'

'She really does.'

Joanne got up and made a pot of tea then brought it to the table.

'I guess you should have a think about what you want as a moving in present then.' Her dad smiled over his mug.

'We haven't even decided if we're going to live at Max's or buy somewhere yet.'

'There's plenty of time for that.' Her dad sipped his tea. 'However, I could do with a hand right now getting the tree down from the attic. We normally get the decorations up earlier, but this year has flown.'

'It really has, hasn't it?'

'Come on then, finish your tea then you can help your old man.'

'You're not old, Dad, just well brewed.'

'Like a good cup of tea, right?'

'Exactly.'

They clinked their mugs together and Joanne smiled. She loved her parents so much and felt lucky to have them, even when her mum was fussing over something or trying to persuade her to do something she had reservations about.

Everything they said and did came down to one thing: it was because they cared.

11

ROXIE

*R*oxie yawned and stretched in bed, smiling as her foot brushed against Fletcher's leg. Their bed was king size, but they still tended to sleep in the middle, touching in one way or another. She'd slept well and felt rested but would lie there for a bit to wake up before going to make them a cup of tea and letting Glenda out. She knew their pug was still sleeping though as she could hear soft little snores coming from the luxury dog basket at the bottom of their bed.

She turned over and gazed at her husband who lay on his front, head turned towards her, arms tucked under his pillow. His salt and pepper hair was sticking up at the back and his short dark eyelashes fluttered on his cheeks. His hairline was receding slowly, but Roxie thought it made him quite distinguished and that he had that Harrison Ford handsomeness about him as he got older. She moved closer to him and placed her hand on his back, savouring his warmth and the smoothness of his skin. It would be so easy to lie here all day and just watch him sleep.

There was no rush today, anyway, was there? They could take their time and have a lazy morning, enjoy breakfast then take a walk.

Hold on. What's the date?

Reaching for her phone, she touched her thumb to the pad and the date and time showed**: 7.05 - 23rd December.**

Something about the date teased at her awareness and she frowned as she set her phone back on the bedside table.

Then it hit her.

Their Christmas party was today!

She sat upright, her heart racing, her hair falling from its bobble and tumbling around her shoulders like an ebony curtain.

'Fletcher. Wake up.'

'Hmm?'

'The party's today.'

'What?'

He rolled over and rubbed his eyes. 'What time is it?'

'Time to get up. We have so much to do today.'

She slid out of bed and went to the window then opened the curtains. Outside, the garden was white. Everything had a thick white covering and snow was still falling, big fat flakes of it drifted down from the sky like squashed marshmallows.

'Oh . . .'

'What's wrong?' Fletcher pushed a hand through is hair, frowning as it stuck up despite his attempts to flatten it.

'It's snowing heavily and . . . the marquee is going to be freezing.'

'Come here.' He held out a hand.

'I can't. I have to figure this out.' She placed a hand on her stomach, feeling its gentle curve beneath the silk of her night-dress, wishing it wasn't rolling quite so much.

'Not yet you don't. Come back to bed and we'll work it out together.'

She glanced at Glenda, smiling in spite of herself at the little dog curled up under a blanket oblivious to it all, then went back to bed.

Fletcher held up the duvet and she climbed in and moved into his embrace. He held her there with her head on his chest, the gentle rise and fall of his breathing and regular beat of his heart soothing her.

'We can dig a path from the back door to the marquee and I have patio heaters to go outside in the garden and some infrared ones to go inside the marquee. We'll give everyone faux fur throws and tell them to wear warm coats and gloves and, don't forget, we can use the house too.'

'But the marquee is meant to be the site of the proposal.'

'And it will be. I promise you. Now don't worry, just rest because it's going to be a busy day.'

She nodded then raised her head to look at him. He smelt incredible. He was so warm and strong as he held her. Something crossed his face and his lips curled upwards.

'Really, Mrs Walker? Is that lust I see in your gaze?'

'Well . . . we're both awake now.'

He pulled her closer and kissed her, and all Roxie's worries faded away as she lost herself in her husband's love.

*A*fter breakfast, the party preparations began in earnest. Roxie and Fletcher donned wellies, coats and gloves and went outside to dig a path from the back door to the marquee. With Glenda running back and forth too, the way was soon cleared and Fletcher turned the heaters on early afternoon to get the marquee warmed up.

During the day, the caterers delivered the party food to the house — luckily they were able to make it because the main roads weren't too bad — and things that needed to be kept cool were placed in the fridge. Fletcher had set up a bar in the marquee with a wine fridge that he'd bought for such occasions. Roxie dug out as many throws as she could find and placed them on the backs of the chairs they'd had delivered the previous day from a local events company.

When Joanne arrived at just after three p.m., she gave Roxie a hand decorating, and soon the marquee resembled a silver Christmas grotto. Ethan had also been around throughout the day, bringing champagne, ice and fifteen small Christmas trees that he arranged outside the front door, through the hallway, along the path to the marquee and inside the marquee, then he decorated them with tiny twinkling fairy lights.

When everything was finally ready, Roxie stood back and smiled.

'We've done a good job.'

'It looks amazing.' Joanne nodded.

Glenda was incredibly excited and kept racing around the marquee, along the garden and into the house then back out again as if she couldn't quite believe what she was seeing.

'Glenda, you need to calm down now or you'll be too tired to enjoy the party.' Fletcher picked her up and stroked her head but she looked at him, tongue hanging from the side of her mouth, eyes bulging.

'You treat her like a child.' Joanne smiled.

'She is our child,' Roxie said as she planted a kiss on Glenda's head.

'Thank you so much for all this.' Ethan cleared his throat. 'I'm so grateful.'

'It's our pleasure.'

'Mum's bringing the cup-cakes along soon. She's been baking for two days.'

'It was a wonderful idea that you had about how to propose,' Roxie said.

'I just hope Lila likes it.'

'She will and her dress is just perfect for this setting.'

Ethan's eyes widened.

'Don't tell me you haven't see the dress yet?' Roxie raised her eyebrows.

'We decided I'd wait until this evening.'

'She looks like a princess in it.' Roxie placed a hand on her chest as the memory of how beautiful Lila had looked in the dress came back.

'I can't wait.' Ethan nodded. 'Right, I'd better go home and get ready. See you just before seven?'

'You will.' Roxie walked him to the door then took his hand. 'This is going to be wonderful.'

'I hope so. I'm very nervous.' He shook his head. 'In fact, I can't believe how nervous I am.'

'Everything will be perfect.' Roxie paused. 'Hold on. I have something I want you to give to Lila. She might need it this evening if she doesn't have one to match her dress.' She hurried upstairs, grabbed a coat from her cupboard then returned to the hallway.

'Here.' She handed it to him.

'Thanks.'

He marched down the driveway through the snow and Roxie closed the door then turned back to admire her hallway. The small Christmas trees looked so pretty with their twinkling lights and she liked how they led the way to the marquee. She understood why Ethan was so nervous but knew he didn't need to be. Lila was going to be delighted by the effort he'd made and the evening would be a lovely way to start Christmas.

12

LILA

*L*ila looked at her reflection. It was her and yet there was something different. The silver dress shimmered as she moved and brushed softly against her skin. Her cheeks were pink and her eyes bright, as if lit from within. She didn't think they used to look this way and wondered if it was being in love and being pregnant. It was as if her body was glowing with its condition and her skin and hair looked better than ever. She'd washed and dried her bobbed blonde hair then pinned one side back with a diamanté clip that Roxie had spotted in a shop in Covent Garden. Her shoes were not so glamorous, a pair of furry sheepskin boots to keep her feet warm, but they were very comfortable. The advantage was that they didn't show under the long skirt, except for the toes that peeped out as she walked, but she didn't mind that. Roxie had also sent a faux fur grey coat home with Ethan and Lila put it on now, admiring how well it did go with her dress, making her look a bit like a winter bride.

She added a slick of pale pink lip gloss then picked up her small silver clutch bag and opened the bedroom door. The thought of Ethan seeing her like this made her feel apprehensive because she wanted him to see her dressed up and to like what he saw.

Downstairs, she took a deep breath then entered the living room.

'Ta da!' She twirled around then smiled, waiting for his reaction.

'You look amazing.' It was Joanne.

'Joanne? Uh . . . hi. Sorry . . . I was expecting Ethan.'

Joanne nodded. 'He said to tell you sorry, but he had to dash off to see a client. Apparently, there was an issue with a job he'd done and the client wanted it sorted asap before Christmas.'

'It's Christmas Eve tomorrow.'

'Exactly.'

'Did he say how long he'd be?'

Joanne shook her head. 'No idea. However, I am here and I can escort you to the party.'

Lila composed herself, swallowing her disappointment. It was silly really, she spent a lot of time with Ethan and he saw her first thing in the morning and last thing at night, on days when she needed to wash her hair and when she had spots. It didn't matter that he wasn't here to see her now, but she would have liked to WOW him.

'I'm sure he'll get there at some point in the evening.' Joanne stood up and crossed the room. 'I've checked on the cats and they're both sleeping so if you grab your gloves and hat, we can get going.'

'Thanks.' Lila nodded then carefully slid her hat over her hair. 'Let's go then.'

She locked the door behind them and walked cautiously down the path, trying to appreciate the snow and how pretty everything looked, but wishing desperately that Ethan wouldn't be late. It was their first Christmas together and it would be the only one before they became parents.

Joanne held out her arm. 'Hold on tight, please, because you're carrying precious cargo now.'

Lila smiled. Thank goodness for her friends.

She tucked her arm through Joanne's and they set off through the winter wonderland known as Wisteria Hollow.

❄

*W*hen they reached Roxie's, they walked up the driveway and Lila's heart squeezed. It was unbelievably beautiful. Snow was falling softly, covering everything in a cold white blanket that seemed to sparkle in the streetlights. This effect was amplified by the fairy lights on the small Christmas trees lining the driveway. Lights also twinkled in the windows of the house and icicles glowed on the edges of the roof while thousands of tiny lights adorned the roof.

'It's breath taking,' Joanne whispered, as if afraid of disturbing the muffled peace that heavy snowfall brought to the small village.

'It really is.'

They reached the porch and were greeted with a loud *HO! HO! HO!*

Lila gasped and Joanne jumped.

'Bloody hell, I wasn't expecting to see that.' Joanne laughed as they stared at the six-foot Santa figure standing next to the front door. 'Roxie could have warned us.'

'She did mention Santa, remember, and his giant—'

'Belly!'

'That's right.'

They both snorted at the memory of how that conversation had gone.

'He must have cost a fortune.' Joanne reached out and touched his beard.

'I bet he did, but you know Roxie, no expense spared when it comes to Christmas.'

Joanne knocked on the door and they waited. Lila's breath emerged in white puffs that disappeared into the icy evening air. She stamped her feet to keep warm and rubbed her tingling nose.

The door opened, and Fletcher grinned at them. He was wearing a bright green Christmas jumper and jeans with heavy snow boots and a red Santa hat.

'Good evening, lovely ladies. Quick, come in out of the cold.'

They stepped inside and the warmth washed over them. The house smelt of cinnamon and gingerbread as well as something savoury.

'Chilly, isn't it?' Fletcher hugged himself as if to illustrate his point.

'Freezing.' Joanne nodded. 'Many here yet?'

He nodded then gave her a wink that Lila thought seemed a bit strange.

'I'm sorry that Ethan isn't here,' Lila said. 'I was getting ready but when I went downstairs, Joanne was there and she told me that Ethan had to rush back to see a client as there was an issue with a job. I'm hoping he won't be long.'

Fletcher smiled but a tiny muscle in his jaw twitched. 'I'm sure he won't. No one's going to keep him away from his friends and partner on Christmas Eve Eve, are they?'

'I hope not.' Lila gave a small shrug and tried to swallow the disappointment that he wasn't here with her now. It was their first Christmas and she'd had ideas about how it would be, but already he'd had to go somewhere else and she was missing him desperately. Perhaps it was pregnancy hormones, but she suddenly felt very vulnerable and as if she might cry.

'Come on through. The marquee is nice and warm because of the heaters and there's plenty of food and drink out there too.'

He led the way and Lila gazed at the Christmas trees in the hallways and through the kitchen.

'It's like a pathway,' she said as she removed her hat and tucked it into a pocket.

'It is.' Fletcher nodded. 'Like it's leading us somewhere special.'

Lila glanced at Joanne and Joanne shrugged as if she was as confused by Fletcher's comment as Lila was.

The kitchen was bright and warm, the aromas of food stronger in there, and Lila looked around. Roxie's kitchen was always a welcoming space but today it seemed even more so with fairy lights on the window and on the large tree in the corner.

'Watch your step outside, because in spite of our attempts to clear a path, it is quite slippery.' Fletcher gestured at the path through the snow that led from the back door to the opening of the marquee.

When they reached the marquee, Fletcher paused, causing Lila and Joanne to stop too. Either side of the opening were ice sculptures. The left one was of two hearts set side by side and the right one was of a couple embracing.

'These are lovely, Fletcher,' Lila said.

'Aren't they? And so appropriate for this evening.'

Lila glanced at Joanne and again, Joanne shrugged.

'Wait here just one moment, please.' He held up a hand then disappeared into the marquee leaving Lila feeling confused.

'What's going on? Do we need to show our IDs to prove our ages?' She giggled.

Joanne smiled. 'That would be funny, wouldn't it?'

'OK, you can come in now.' Fletcher stood back and gestured for them to walk inside.

It took a moment for Lila's eyes to adjust because it was darker in the marquee than outside, but then she realised that lots of people were standing around with drinks and that they were all looking her way.

'Joanne. What's going on?'

Joanne took her hand. 'It's fine, sweetheart. Just go with it.'

Lila's eyes moved over the people and she spotted Roxie, who was smiling and waving, Ethan's mum, Freda, Max, yoga teacher Finlay Bridgewater and others from the village. Fletcher had been right; the marquee was warm and cosy and it resembled a festive grotto with more of the Christmas trees that she'd seen on the driveway and in the house dotted around and tiny lights draped around the periphery. There was a bar in the one corner, tables and chairs set around in groups, and then, at the centre of it all was a space and in that space stood Ethan.

'What's going on?' she asked, raising her voice slightly so he could hear her. 'I thought you were with a client?'

'Sorry about that, but I needed to get here before you.'

'But why?'

'See all this?' He waved his arms to encompass the marquee, the people, the champagne that Roxie was pouring into flutes. 'It's for you.'

'For me?'

He nodded.

'Go to him.' Joanne gave her a gentle nudge in the small of her back, so Lila walked towards Ethan, smiling at their friends as she passed them, feeling uncertain yet excited.

She reached him and he took her hands in his then raised them to his lips. Lila realised he was wearing a suit she hadn't seen before, a charcoal grey one with a sheen to the material and a silver tie. He looked very handsome and very smart.

'I love you, Lila. I have loved you since the first day I saw you. You're an incredible woman and have quickly become my best friend and my world. We have a bright and wonderful future ahead of us and I know with all my heart that I want to be with you for the rest of my life.'

Lila gasped. Her heart was racing and her head felt light. She had a sensation of floating, as if this wasn't real, and yet it was. Her boots were anchoring her to the wooden boards, Ethan's hands were anchoring her to him, and the smiling faces of their friends were there to confirm that this was really happening.

'Lila . . .' Ethan released one of her hands then moved his to his jacket pocket and pulled out a ring. 'Will you spend your life with me?'

She gazed at him, her eyes following the familiar line of his jaw, his broad shoulders, the mole on his left earlobe that she liked to kiss. The few greys in the sides of his hair caught the light and his eyes seemed so dark she could have fallen into them.

She loved this man with every fibre of her being and nothing would make her happier than to spend her life with him.

'Yes please,' she said softly, her throat tightening with emotion.

'What was that?' someone shouted from the back of the onlookers.

Ethan smiled. 'Can you say it louder for the man at the back?'

'Yes! A thousand times yes!'

Ethan slid the ring onto her finger, and she held it up to the light. It was a silver band with a princess cut diamond at the centre.

'It's so beautiful,' she said.

'Just like you.'

Ethan swept her into his arms and kissed her and around them everyone cheered and clapped and somewhere, Glenda barked.

13

ROXIE

*W*hen Ethan and Lila finally stopped kissing, Roxie went over and hugged them both then lifted Lila's hand so she could admire the ring.

'Well look at that. Isn't it gorgeous?'

'I can't believe it.' Lila was gazing at the ring as if starstruck. 'I'm engaged.'

Fletcher came over and congratulated Ethan, clapping him heartily on the back and concern filled Roxie as Lila's face slowly changed from one of joy to one of sadness.

'What is it?' she whispered as she leant closer.

Lila met her eyes. 'What if . . .'

Roxie shook her head. 'It won't happen again, sweetheart. Ethan loves you and wanted to show you. That's why he did all this.' She raised her hands and gestured at the marquee. 'He wanted you to know that this is for keeps. He loves you and the baby you're carrying and he won't let you down. I know it.'

'He won't?'

'No he won't.' Roxie hugged Lila then kissed her cheek. 'So just enjoy this evening and celebrate your love for Ethan and the wonderful future you're going to have.'

Lila smiled and it lit up her face. 'Thank you. I don't know what I'd do without you.'

'Ditto.' Roxie had to swallow hard as emotion rose in her throat. 'Right I'd better stop being sentimental because I do not want to ruin my mascara.' She winked at Lila then turned back to Ethan and Fletcher. 'I think we need to open some more fizz, husband dear, don't you?'

'Absolutely, my darling wife.' Fletcher tapped his Santa hat then made his way over to the bar.

'I'm so happy for you both.' Joanne had joined them and she was grinning. 'What a fabulous start to Christmas. Let me see that ring, Lila.'

Lila held out her hand and Joanne turned it from side to side, so the diamond caught the light. Then Freda came to admire it and soon Lila was surrounded by women commenting on the ring and enveloping Lila in perfume scented hugs.

Roxie stepped back and watched, pride filling her chest as if Lila was her own child. There wasn't much between them age wise, only seventeen years, but sometimes she felt a lot older than Lila and very protective of her. They'd joked in the past that Roxie could be Lila's older sister, but for Roxie, sometimes she felt more like she could be Lila's foster mother.

Excitement rushed through her as she realised that this would mean there would be a wedding to plan, which meant a dress to buy, things to organise and possibly all before baby arrived. It would be a busy time following Christmas but Roxie like being busy and, while she wouldn't interfere, she'd help wherever she was needed.

But first, she'd help her husband to replenish everyone's glasses.

'Here you go,' Fletcher said as he handed Roxie a fresh glass of champagne after they'd catered to their guests, then clinked his own against it. 'To a good party.'

'The night is young yet.' Roxie looked around the marquee at people talking, eating, dancing and smiling. 'I think there's a lot of celebrating to be done.'

'It's a good job we stocked up on bubbly then.' He slid an arm around her waist. 'Are you happy, Roxie?'

'Incredibly happy. I was just thinking about how it's like having a daughter.'

He knitted his brows. 'What is?'

'Well . . . Lila. She's one of my best friends but she's also the closest thing I have to a sister or a daughter.'

'You're not old enough to be her mum.'

'I am . . . and I feel old enough some days.' She smiled and he smiled too.

'You're the hottest woman I've ever seen and the only woman I want.'

'You always say the right thing.'

She leant her head on him and sighed with contentment. It had been a busy year but also a good one and everything seemed to be going to plan.

14

ROXIE

ood morning sleepy head.' Roxie opened her eyes as Fletcher kissed her lips, her cheeks, her forehead. 'Merry Christmas.'

She smiled at him and stretched, savouring the bed warmth and her husband's kisses.

'Merry Christmas.'

'I've brought you a cup of tea but when we go downstairs, I'll make you a Bellini.'

'You're the best.'

She sat up and pushed her hair back from her face.

'I try.' He shrugged then climbed into bed next to her.

'What time is it?'

'After eight.'

'I slept like a log.'

'We both did. I got up about an hour ago because there was a delivery.'

'On Christmas Day?'

He nodded. 'Strange, I know.'

'What is it?'

'You'll have to come down and see for yourself.'

She frowned. 'Where's Glenda?'

'Playing with the delivery.'

'Oh god . . . it's not edible is it?'

Fletcher raised his eyebrows. 'I hope not.'

'Phew. Is it for both of us?'

'Yes, and for Glenda. It's something we've needed for a while.'

Roxie picked up her tea and sipped it. 'That's what I call a good cup of Earl Grey.'

'Want to go down yet?' Fletcher was grinning at her like he'd just won the lottery.

'You're behaving strangely. You're almost fifty not five, so what's the hurry? It's not like the delivery was from Santa, is it?'

'No . . . but I don't like to leave it downstairs on its own.'

'You're teasing now right?' She finished her tea then swung back the quilt and got out of bed. Reaching for her fluffy dressing gown, she put it on then went to the ensuite. 'I'll just be a minute.'

When she returned to the bedroom, Fletcher was waiting with the empty mugs.

'Ready?'

'I am.' She placed a hand on his arm. 'Don't forget to remind me to put the turkey in soon.'

'I won't. Seeing as how we have *more* guests coming now.'

Roxie laughed. When Lila and Ethan had been leaving after the party, she'd invited them to Christmas dinner. Ethan had smiled then his face had fallen. He'd said he couldn't possibly come and leave his mum home alone. Roxie had told him that of course she meant his mum too; she'd never leave anyone out. Lila had been very grateful, looked relieved to be able to rest and not have to cook dinner and Freda had been delighted when they told her. She'd phoned Roxie on Christmas Eve and asked what she could do to help. Roxie's mum and dad were also coming for dinner and she was looking forward to seeing them and sharing all the recent news over turkey and stuffing.

Downstairs, Roxie paused and looked around. The trees Ethan had brought were still there but arranged at the edges of the hall to create more space and the lights on them twinkled prettily. The scent of pine filled the air and it made her think of Christmases gone by, of happy times spent with family and friends. It was such a lovely time of year and she always enjoyed it, had even enjoyed those times when it had just been her and Fletcher, because all they'd ever needed was each other, but being with other loved ones was icing on the Christmas cake.

A bark came from the kitchen followed by another one, and Roxie tilted her head, thinking that it was strange for Glenda to be barking when she was alone. She often barked in play and when she was excited so this was unusual.

Roxie hurried through the hallway but when she got to the kitchen, she was surprised to find a safety gate blocking her way.

'Fletcher what is this? Why have you blocked Glenda in there alone?'

She fiddled with the lock on the gate, desperate to get through to her little dog, feeling confused about what her husband was playing at. Had he gone completely mad?

He reached around her and pressed a button on the handle and it swung open.

'It's just temporary to keep the delivery safe.' He gestured for her to go through.

'Glenda!' Roxie looked around and there, under the table, was her baby girl. 'There you are. Come to Mummy.' She crouched down and Glenda turned and looked at her but then she turned back to the table again. 'Glenda, what is it?'

There was a bark, but it wasn't Glenda. Roxie crawled over to the table and peered underneath.

'Oh . . . Hello.'

Under the table, peering out at her, was a small black dog.

She held out her hand and Glenda came to her, tiny tail wagging then sat at her side as if to wait for their guest to emerge.

'Who is this, Fletcher?'

He knelt next to her.

'This, my darling, is Stinky.'

'Stinky?' Roxie frowned at the name, but the dog ran towards her and jumped onto her lap. She wrapped her arms around it and stroked its head. 'What kind of name is that?'

'It started as a joke apparently because Stinky had some stinky wind. A woman I used to work with had her . . . she's a Yorkipoo.'

Roxie gazed at the ball of black fur in her lap that was gazing up at her with dark eyes filled with understanding.

'She's beautiful.'

Glenda sniffed at Stinky's ears, nose and bottom.

'Glenda! Get your nose away from there.'

Glenda pawed at Roxie's arm.

'I think our little girl will need some time to get used to not being the only baby in the house.'

'What do you mean?'

'Well . . . as long as you're happy . . . Stinky can stay with us.'

'All the time?'

He nodded. 'Not just as a visitor. My ex colleague had her last year as a gift from her boyfriend, but they split up in the summer and she's just got a contract to work in Dubai. She didn't want to take Stinky because she'd have to leave the dog home alone while she's out at work all day, and she also didn't want to put her through the trauma of the flight. She sent out an email asking if anyone was looking for a dog and asked that anyone interested be serious about wanting a dog because Stinky is a very special girl. I replied telling her I thought it would be good for Glenda and for us, then went to meet her in London and when I met Stinky, I thought she was very cute and would be a great addition to our family. She's a sweet little thing and very loyal and loving.'

'She's adorable.'

'Glenda likes her.'

'Glenda likes everyone.' Roxie shifted her position to sit cross legged on the floor and Glenda climbed over her leg to sit next to Stinky. 'But what an awful name.'

Fletcher laughed.

'I guess we can't really change it now seeing as how she's had it for a year.'

'I guess not.'

'Let's keep her then and her daft name.'

'Thank goodness for that!' He squeezed Roxie's shoulder. 'She's your gift and Glenda's gift. I've got you the usual things . . . jewellery, lingerie and some other surprises but I thought it would be nice to have another little dog around the place.'

'It will be good for us all.' Roxie kissed him. 'Has she had breakfast?'

He nodded. 'Robin said she'd fed her a small breakfast before they set out, but it'll be good for her to eat with Glenda and to start her new routine.'

'I hope she'll be OK. What if she misses her mum?'

Fletcher hugged Roxie with one arm, and he took turns stroking Glenda and Stinky with his other hand. They both gazed up at him adoringly.

'You're her mum now, Roxie, and I'm sure she'll be happy here with us.'

Roxie nodded. 'We'll do everything we can to make you happy, Stinky.'

'Shall we have a Bellini now?' Fletcher asked as he stood up.

'That's a good plan.'

Roxie slowly got up and the dogs stood too.

'Either of you need a wee?' she asked.

Glenda barked and Stinky copied her, so Roxie opened the back door and let them out. Fletcher handed her a champagne flute and they stood in the doorway in their pyjamas and dressing gowns, laughing as the dogs raced around the outside of the marquee, leaving tiny paw prints in the crisp white snow.

Roxie knew that they would all need to make adjustments and that it would take time for Stinky to settle in, but she was part of their family now and she'd soon understand that.

'Right, my love, let's get that turkey in the oven.' Roxie set her glass on the worktop then rolled up her sleeves.

'And I'll start on the sprouts.'

Fletcher got the colander out of a cupboard while Roxie went to the fridge and got out the turkey she'd prepared the night before, smothering butter under the skin, layering streaky bacon over the outside and filling it with apricot and hazelnut stuffing.

It was going to be a very merry Christmas indeed.

Joanne

'So what do you think?' Max asked Joanne as they sat snuggled on the sofa at her parents' house. Her long legs were draped over his with her laptop balanced on them. They'd been looking at houses that were for sale in the village.

'I'm not sure. Both houses look nice but it's such a big decision.'

His dark brown eyes held her gaze and she felt herself getting lightheaded. This kept happening when he gazed at her so intently.

'It is.' He smiled. 'Or . . . we can just stay at my place for a while until we find a property we really love.'

She closed the laptop and put it on the coffee table then wrapped her arms around his neck.

'That does sound like a good plan. I like the houses we've seen but we also haven't done anything else yet.'

'Like what?'

'Been on a holiday. Isn't there somewhere you'd like to go next year?'

'Are you thinking beach holiday or cultural?'

'I'm not a big sunbather with my fair skin. I like good weather, but I also like learning about places.'

'How about New York? Ever been there?'

She shook her head.

'We could go.'

Excitement shot through Joanne and she grinned. 'Really?'

Max nodded. 'If you move into my house, we can save for a deposit on a place while also enjoying some holidays.'

'That sounds like a brilliant plan.'

'That's settled then. Let's enjoy today then from tomorrow we can start looking for a holiday. You'll love Manhattan.'

'I can't wait!' She kissed him, losing herself in his embrace then jumped as someone cleared their throat.

'Uh . . . Joanne. Kerry and Jeremy just pulled up outside.'

Joanne slid her legs off Max's and straightened her sparkly tunic top.

'OK, Dad, thanks.'

Her dad hovered in the doorway then left the room and Joanne stood up, giggling. 'Poor Dad, he didn't need to see that.'

Max's cheeks were flushed. 'He didn't. How embarrassing. I won't be able to look at him over the roasties.'

Joanne shook her head. 'He'll be fine. He's already had three sherries and two glasses of champagne.'

There was a knock at the front door.

'Merry Christmas!' her dad called from the hallway and she heard her sister and brother-in-law along with their children as they came inside.

'How are you feeling?' she asked Max. 'The children will be very excited.'

He nodded. 'I'm bracing myself.'

They went to the doorway and Max took Joanne's hand, entwining his fingers with hers. She could tell that he was a bit nervous and understood why. She was nervous too, about how he would find her family and how they would get on. If there was ever a test of compatibility, it was a family Christmas. But then Max was so friendly, calm and easy going that she felt sure he would be fine and that her family would love him as much as she did. Her mum and dad already did love him, but today he'd spend an extended amount of time with Kerry and Jeremy as well as with her niece and nephew.

'Ready?' she asked him.

'Ready.' He smiled then she gave him a quick kiss for luck, and they walked out to enjoy their first Christmas together.

Roxie

'*H*ello darling.' Roxie hugged Lila in the hallway after she'd taken their coats then leant back and gazed at Lila's middle. 'I swear you look a bit rounder today.'

Lila giggled. 'It's all the mince pies Freda keeps making.' She patted her belly.

'I have to feed you up, Lila, you're keeping my grandchild warm.' Freda smiled and Roxie admired how well she was looking. Freda hadn't been well back in the spring and had been suffering from angina, but she'd had a blocked artery cleared and a stent put in and her health had improved. She'd always been fit and did yoga and pilates at the village hall but like everyone, she was only human.

'You look wonderful, Freda,' Roxie said.

'Thank you, Roxie. Lila bought this blouse for me for Christmas and I really like it.' The gold silk blouse seemed to make her skin glow and looked very smart with black trousers and black leather boots. Freda had always been wiry as she used to run and the yoga and Pilates kept her toned, but her figure seemed a bit softer, her cheeks a bit fuller and it suited her with her short grey pixie cut.

'And hello Ethan.'

'Merry Christmas, Roxie.' He kissed her cheeks, a broad grin never leaving his face.

'Something smells good,' Lila said.

'Everything's cooking away so all we need to do now is open some champagne.' Roxie smiled then looked at Lila. 'Or orange juice for you.'

'It's OK, we've got that covered.' Ethan raised a Christmas gift bag that he was carrying. 'There's some non-alcoholic fizz in here for the pregnant lady.'

'Perfect.' Roxie clapped her hands. 'Come on through.'

She made to unlock the safety gate in the kitchen doorway then paused.

'One thing . . . this is here because we have a new addition to our family. Fletcher and I have adopted a little dog from a former colleague of his who's moving away. The dog is just adorable, but we need to keep this closed for now to stop her and Glenda racing around the house.'

'You've adopted another dog?' Lila asked, her eyebrows raised.

'Yes. Fletcher said that it would be good for Glenda to have some canine company and I agree. She's a Yorkipoo and only just over a year old.'

'What's her name?' Ethan asked.

Roxie sucked in a deep breath. 'Stinky.'

'Stinky?' Freda laughed. 'Who calls their dog Stinky?'

'I know.' Roxie shook her head. 'But she's used to it now and I don't think we can change it.'

She opened the gate and they followed her through to the kitchen where Fletcher was setting glasses out on the breakfast bar.

'Merry Christmas!' Fletcher said as he turned to their guests then greeted them individually before showing them to the table.

'Where are the dogs?' Roxie asked.

Fletcher nodded at the back door so Roxie peered outside. Glenda and Stinky were roaming around the marquee, sniffing at the edges and at the snowy lawn. Glenda was clearly leading the way and the younger dog was following her lead, watching her carefully and imitating her actions.

'They seem to have made friends, Fletcher.' She placed a hand over her chest. 'That's the cutest thing.'

He joined her at the door. 'I know. I thought it would be good for Glenda because as much as she loves us, she now has someone else to play with.' He handed Roxie a glass of champagne. 'Come and say Merry Christmas to your guests.'

Fletcher took hold of Roxie's hand and led her over to the table. It was laid with a silver and white tablecloth, silver napkins and gold Christmas crackers. At the middle of the rectangular table, a thick white candle set in the centre of a holly wreath burned and the light reflected on the glassware set out for wine and water.

'This is all so beautiful.' Lila sniffed. 'Thank you.'

Ethan took her hand. 'I think the hormones are kicking in, don't you?'

Lila nodded. 'But it's not just that. A year ago, my life was very different. I had Roxie and Joanne but I'd been through such a low time and I was quite unhappy. I never could have dreamt that this Christmas I'd have a new partner, a mother-in-law in all but name and a baby on the way. It's like all my Christmas wishes came true at once.'

Her eyes glistened as she gazed around the table and Roxie's throat tightened. She blinked hard and breathed slowly to try to control her emotions because she felt that if she started to cry, she'd struggle to stop. But she didn't feel sad or unhappy, just incredibly glad that everything had worked out.

When she felt able to speak, she raised her glass of champagne.

'I'd like to make a toast.' She met everyone's eyes in turn. 'To all of you for making this year a wonderful one. To Fletcher for being the best husband a woman could have, for being the love of my life and for being my world. To Freda, for being there for Ethan and for Lila and for being an inspiration, especially at yoga. To Ethan for making Lila a very happy woman and for being a very lovely friend to us. And finally, to Lila. You are the sweetest kindest person I know, and I'm honoured to call you my friend. To see you with Ethan and Freda, safely ensconced in a loving family makes me happier than I can explain. You deserve to be happy and I am sure that you have a wonderful future ahead of you now and I cannot wait to be an aunty.' She sipped her drink, fighting tears again.

'Thank you Roxie with all of my heart.' Lila's cheeks were wet now but she was smiling and Ethan had wrapped an arm around her shoulders.

'There's something I've always believed,' Roxie smiled at Lila. 'We can have family we're related to by blood and love them deeply. But if we're lucky, we have something extra special and that's good friends. Whether we have blood family or not, our friends are, without a doubt, the family we choose for ourselves.'

Just then, the doorbell rang.

'Talking of blood relatives, that will be Mum and Dad.'

Roxie got up and went to the front door to let her parents in, two small dogs at her heels as they'd sneaked through the safety gate when she opened it.

Now that her parents had arrived, the celebrations could properly begin and there was so much good news to share. Roxie knew that this year, her Christmas wishes really had come true.

THE END

DEAR READER

Thank you so much for reading *Christmas Wishes on Sunflower Street*. I hope you enjoyed the story.

If you can spare five minutes of your time, I would be so grateful if you could leave a rating and a short review.

You can find me on Twitter **@authorRG,** on Facebook at **Rachel Griffiths Author** and on Instagram at **rachelgriffithsauthor** if you'd like to connect with me to find out more about my books and what I'll be working on next.

With love,
Rachel X

ABOUT THE AUTHOR

Rachel Griffiths is an author, wife, mother, Earl Grey tea drinker, gin enthusiast, dog walker and fan of the afternoon nap. She loves to read, write and spend time with her family.

ALSO BY RACHEL GRIFFITHS

CWTCH COVE SERIES

CHRISTMAS AT CWTCH COVE

WINTER WISHES AT CWTCH COVE

MISTLETOE KISSES AT CWTCH COVE

THE COTTAGE AT CWTCH COVE

THE CAFÉ AT CWTCH COVE

CAKE AND CONFETTI AT CWTCH COVE

A NEW ARRIVAL AT CWTCH COVE

THE COSY COTTAGE CAFÉ SERIES

SUMMER AT THE COSY COTTAGE CAFÉ

AUTUMN AT THE COSY COTTAGE CAFÉ

WINTER AT THE COSY COTTAGE CAFÉ

SPRING AT THE COSY COTTAGE CAFÉ

A WEDDING AT THE COSY COTTAGE CAFÉ

A YEAR AT THE COSY COTTAGE CAFÉ (THE COMPLETE SERIES)

THE LITTLE CORNISH GIFT SHOP SERIES

CHRISTMAS AT THE LITTLE CORNISH GIFT SHOP

SPRING AT THE LITTLE CORNISH GIFT SHOP

SUMMER AT THE LITTLE CORNISH GIFT SHOP

THE LITTLE CORNISH GIFT SHOP (THE COMPLETE SERIES)

SUNFLOWER STREET SERIES

SPRING SHOOTS ON SUNFLOWER STREET

SUMMER DAYS ON SUNFLOWER STREET

AUTUMN SPICE ON SUNFLOWER STREET

CHRISTMAS WISHES ON SUNFLOWER STREET

A WEDDING ON SUNFLOWER STREET

A NEW BABY ON SUNFLOWER STREET

NEW BEGINNINGS ON SUNFLOWER STREET

SNOWFLAKES AND CHRISTMAS CAKES ON SUNFLOWER STREET

A YEAR ON SUNFLOWER STREET (SUNFLOWER STREET BOOKS 1-4)

THE COSY COTTAGE ON SUNFLOWER STREET

SNOWED IN ON SUNFLOWER STREET

SPRINGTIME SURPRISES ON SUNFLOWER STREET

AUTUMN DREAMS ON SUNFLOWER STREET

A CHRISTMAS TO REMEMBER ON SUNFLOWER STREET

STANDALONE STORIES

CHRISTMAS AT THE LITTLE COTTAGE BY THE SEA

THE WEDDING

ACKNOWLEDGMENTS

Thanks go to:

My gorgeous family. I love you so much! XXX

My author and blogger friends, for your support, advice and encouragement.

Everyone who buys, reads and reviews this book.

Printed in Great Britain
by Amazon